TheEremite

David Cloet

ISBN No: 978-1-903172-77-3

Publishers: Barny Books
              Hough on the Hill,
              Grantham,
              Lincolnshire
              NG32 2BB

              Tel: 01400 250246
              www.barnybooks.biz

Printers: Athenaeum Press Ltd
              Dukesway
              Team Valley
              Gateshead
              Tyne & Wear
              NE11 0PZ

For

Christopher, Craig, Paul and Shaun

also

Charlotte and Fleur,
Sam James, Natalie and Olivia
Amber, Megan and Samuel Henry

Not forgetting

Ockert, Casper and Joshua

Dedication

The Pattaya Orphanage Trust

Part One

1933 - 1958

Introduction

It was the first day of the month when Emilia Aarden conceived. By the end of the month Emilia suspected she was pregnant with her third child. She hoped that it would be a boy this time.

In the same month, President Hindenburg appointed Hitler as the Chancellor of Germany.

October 1933
The gestation period complete, the child within Emilia's womb entered the world on the 7th of the month. It was a boy. On the 22nd he was baptised into the Roman Catholic Church and named after his grandfather, Achille.

Hitler's Third Reich was beginning to become known to the world. Cardinal Faulhaber spoke out against the Nazi party's anti-Christian stance.

The leader in the *Daily Express* on the 7th didn't mention Achille's birth. It was concerned with much more important events, the Irish question in general and the rioting in Tralee in particular.

What is noteworthy however, is the fact that Hitler's decision to withdraw Germany from the League of Nations was only given seven and a half column-inches and that was relegated to page eleven!

So in the nine months that Achille formed in his mother's womb, Hitler spawned his evil regime.

One

Heinz Gasser was a blond, blue-eyed baby, born at the end of the First World War in November 1918. Cunning but not too bright academically, he grew into a well-built young man who became a bully at school. At the age of fifteen he was on the verge of criminality but Hitler's appointment as Chancellor, gave him a sense of direction. Heinz was a natural acolyte.

The opening of the Dachau concentration camp and the rounding up of dissidents in March 1933, met with his approval. The official boycotting of Jewish shops and professional men appealed to his bullyboy nature. When being Aryan was made a pre-condition of pubic office in November 1936, he knew he had a place in this Germany. He joined the army the day after his eighteenth birthday.

He was seen as a keen soldier with good leadership potential. He responded well to the discipline and when he'd completed his training, he was sent to Spain. On March 7th 1938 he became part of the Nationalist drive through Aragon and Castellon, down the Ebro valley. One hundred thousand troops, two hundred tanks and almost one thousand German and Italian aircraft were involved. They drove all before them and reached the sea by April 15th.

He had proved his potential and was returned to Germany in January 1939. He'd done all that was asked of him, acted without conscience and saw Franco as an ally that could help build the Third Reich. His six-year meteoric rise took a fateful step when he was appointed colonel in the SS in August 1939.

Whilst in Spain he had noted Hitler's order that all Jewish wealth must be registered. On his return to Germany, when the order to confiscate all Jewish valuables was issued in April '39, his latent avarice started to occupy his mind.

Hitler invaded Russia in June '41, the 900-day siege of Leningrad began in September but, by December, the German advance had faltered in the Russian winter when they were only thirty miles from Moscow. Also in December, Japan attacked Pearl Harbour, bringing America into the war. By the following April the Americans were helping the British. Colonel Gasser, at an entirely personal level, already began to have secret doubts about the invincibility of Germany.

When the mass gassing of Jews began at Auschwitz in June of '42, he realised they could never reclaim their assets. Now was the time to make his move. He knew instinctively that if he secretly confiscated Jewish assets, his chances of getting caught would diminish as the German hierarchy tried to stem the growing reality of defeat.

In the three months since America had entered the war, he had looked carefully at all the men in his command. As his plan to hide the stolen wealth in Switzerland clarified in his mind, he had picked out Klaus Mecklenbeck, Otto Altmann, Wolfgang Fritz and Wolfgang Mack as the key members of his team.

He approached each in turn with his ideas, knowing he

would kill them if any doubts were expressed. None were. He had chosen well. They in turn each recruited one additional man, approaching them on a similar basis to that adopted by Colonel Gasser. The team of nine, led by Heinz, made detailed plans; which proved to be vastly better than their wildest dreams.

****

Two

Ulrich Hoffman, a cryptographer in the Swiss Diplomatic Service, was recalled from London in March '39, when Germany occupied Bohemia and Moravia. His services were required in Madrid to help assess how Spain, under Franco, would settle down in the aftermath of civil war.

It was a very difficult time for the Spaniards. The start of Franco's thirty-eight year dictatorship had begun brutally. Four hundred thousand Spaniards had been killed in the Civil War, now one million spent time in prison or labour camps and, between '39 and '43, a further one hundred thousand were to be executed.

Ulrich disliked his time in Spain and was happy to be recalled for retraining in December 1941. At a diplomatic reception in Switzerland, Ulrich was astounded to see Maureen Alcock across the room. His heart leapt. They had parted under something of a cloud when he left London in March '39. They had argued over her approach to him on behalf of the British, attempting to capitalise on their burgeoning relationship, perhaps even compromise him?

After his first-hand experience of a brutal regime in Spain and his intense dislike of the Third Reich, he realised he still loved and wanted her. He was now prepared to do as the British had asked.

She still loved him. She had agreed to be posted to Berne as a multi-lingual secretary in the hope that their love might be re-kindled. Her superiors hoped that his attitude might have changed as the brutality of the German regime became ever more apparent.

They fell into each other's arms as far as a diplomatic function would allow. They began going out together again realising how much they had missed each other. They were in love. It was he who broached the subject of their earlier disagreement, saying that as the Swiss were neutral, it was the only way he could do something positive against the Germans. Maureen was delighted that he still felt the same about her and was pleased by the turn of events. They planned to work together passing whatever he was able to discover on to the British.

It was clear to Ulrich from his training, that a posting to Berlin was probable. He and Maureen worked out how they would communicate once he was in place. They became secretly engaged, agreeing they would marry as soon as the war was over.

Ulrich was posted to the Swiss Legation in Berlin in September '42, the month the Germans entered Stalingrad. He returned to Switzerland in December 1944 and was married seven months later in July 1945; two months after the war had ended.

****

Young Achille, then nine, got on well with his parish priest Monsignor Barton. He walked alone to church each weekday morning to serve mass at 7.00am. He returned home for breakfast and then walked to school, where he was progressing well.

He was not overtly religious but thought deeply about the actions of the priest at mass, such as putting water in the wine at the offertory. It reminded him about the wedding feast at Cana where Jesus turned water into wine. The consecration reminded him that when Jesus died on the cross, a Centurion pierced his side with a spear and out came blood and water.

At his age he could not see the adult picture of the role played by a priest in so many aspects of people's lives. He simply admired and respected the position the priest held.

Archbishop Griffin of the Westminster Diocese came in February '45, when a number of eleven-year-old children were

Confirmed. Achille had begun to feel that he might like to become a priest himself and voiced his feeling to his parents.

They discussed this turn of events with Monsignor Barton who agreed that it was possible but far too early to be sure; none-the-less he would make enquiries. He came back to Bruno and Emilia with the fact that such possibilities were catered for but it would mean Achille going away to boarding school. They had reservations about that but Achille wanted to go.

The end of the war in Europe came in May 1945. The prospect of a lasting peace beckoned although rationing would continue for some time yet. The Thousand-Year Reich of Hitler's imagination was crushed in twelve: his reach proving too great for his grasp.

In September of that year Achille went to St Edmunds College, the oldest Catholic public school in England, which also housed Allen Hall, the seminary of the Westminster Diocese.

****

The turning point of the war came when the advance of German troops faltered outside Moscow. The Russian troops began to push them back in December. Hitler realised that the war was lost militarily so he played for time, hoping a new weapon or diplomacy might still save the situation.

Colonel Gasser's team had been very successful in hiding Jewish assets in Switzerland. So in October of '44 he spoke to each member of his team. He gave them sufficient funds to obtain sets of documents, suggesting they make plans for their escape when Germany was defeated and make for Argentina.

In the April and May of 1945, midst the utter confusion which was the turmoil at war's end, each of the team made their escape, making their way to Argentina by a variety of routes.

Heinz Gasser travelled alone. He made for Spain knowing he could count on a couple of friends he'd made there during the civil war and the pro-Axis stance of the Franco regime. He stayed a while until things had quietened down and he could safely get a passage to Buenos Aires, where he arrived in November '45.

Wolfgang Fritz had persuaded his younger brother Herman, who was a test pilot in the Luftwaffe, to join in his escape. By means of a very heavy bribe, Herman flew them direct to Eire in an Arado Ar 234B-Os, called a Blitz, in early May after Hitler had committed suicide. It was an early turbo-jet, with a speed of 460 mph and a ceiling of almost 20,000ft. It was a dangerous undertaking but careful route planning, combined with their speed and height, made for success. They arrived in Argentina, via Eire, in September 1945.

Klaus Mecklenbeck adopted a very different approach. He took his wife and two children into Switzerland posing as refugees. From there they made their way to Argentina, arriving in February 1946.

Wolfgang Mack committed murder to assume a new identity and emigrated to Argentina in due course.

Otto Altmann never revealed how he got to Argentina. Being a homosexual, he was very practiced at keeping secrets. He made contact with Colonel Gasser in January '46.

Heinz Gasser organised for the five of them to get together for an informal meeting in March '46.

"We were fortunate," he said, "Wolfgang Mack who organised the Swiss end of our plan and myself, were able to bring bankers drafts with us, with which we have now opened two bank accounts.

"I cannot over-emphasise the need for tight security. There's a great deal of money at stake. We will pay ourselves a monthly sum to live normal lives and do our homework for the next three months so that we can decide what businesses we want to buy into. We'll meet again in June to discuss and decide on each of our proposals.

"Whilst the sum we have is ample for our needs, you will remember that one of the records went missing towards the end of December 1944. This we must find. It gives the number of the Swiss bank security box that contains the authorisation documents for a series of accounts and deposits. The contents are worth many millions of Swiss Francs. I want you to think how best we can recover those funds as well."

Blending into the general population proved easy enough. In the ninety-year period up to 1940, over six and a half million Europeans had settled in Argentina. The June meeting was held, as if by accident, in La Plata, the five pretending to be on holiday.

At that meeting it was agreed that they buy into five different businesses to spread the investment risk. Their holdings varied from 25% to 49%, depending on the size of the business. None exceeded 49%. They had to learn the business, a controlling interest might prove fatal.

The second subject concerned the recovery of the further funds. Wolfgang Mack agreed to go to Switzerland as a businessman, the first of them to get a valid Argentinean passport. They also agreed to buy, or set up, a private detective agency in Switzerland. It would be largely self-financing and provide valid cover for their enquiries.

****

Three

By the time Achille was in his fourth term at St Edmunds, he was past being homesick and had come to like the daily routine of the college. One afternoon he was asked to go to his housemaster's rooms.

Fr. Purney sat him down to tell him, as gently as he could, that his father had collapsed at work and died a few hours later, without recovering consciousness. He went on to say that his parish priest would collect him by car the following day, to take him home.

He told Achille he need not attend classes or evening prep for the rest of the day and asked him which of his friends he would like to be with him. Having called Alan Walton, the two went for a walk in the grounds, talking about whatever came to mind. At the age of thirteen, Achille was dry-eyed. The loss of his father had not really sunk in. He didn't cry until his mother hugged him the following day when he got home, then his eyes brimmed over as the realization suddenly struck him.

It was a somber, red-eyed household with little said between him, his mother and three sisters, all were preoccupied with their own thoughts. Six days later he served at the requiem mass for his father, then all the family's relatives and friends walked behind the hearse for the short distance to the cemetery. His father was interred, joined his mother Emma, Achilles grandmother, who had died before he was born.

He became more devout over the next few years. The college routine of mass each morning before breakfast and a sung High Mass on Sundays was largely responsible. At High Mass each week the schoolboys were joined by the seminarians from Allen Hall. Achille often recalled the way the seminaries left by filing out, with their cassocks swaying in unison to the stirring music of Widor's toccata and fugue from his fifth organ symphony.

In the summer holidays he usually went to Belgium for two weeks to stay with his grandfather in Loppem, a small village near Bruges. This was to try to improve his French but everyone he met wanted to practice their English. His grandfather was a very devout man. They went to mass each morning before breakfast where grandfather usually served at mass. Whilst Achille was there he took his place. After breakfast, they'd sometimes walk for a couple of kilometers across fields to the Cistercian monastery to attend sung mass, the sound of the monks plainchant was beautiful, a sound that stayed with Achille all his life.

As Achille grew older he started to become troubled and confused. He even began to have doubts about his vocation. He was an ardent Catholic by this time, steeped in the practice of his religion, happy with the prospect of life as a priest but for one thing – young women. The vow of celibacy taken by a priest was something with which he thought he would have great difficulty.

Ever more frequently he'd have carnal thoughts about young women, yet he knew that fornication was a sin. It caused him to blush in the presence of girls. He was too embarrassed to even think of discussing his problem with anyone; his reading of the Catechism led him to believe that even harbouring such thoughts was sinful. It so suffused his mind; his very faith was being challenged. He began to have serious doubts that he could control such lust, particularly if he ever became a priest. He wrestled with this problem for some considerable time. Finally, during the Christmas holidays of 1949, when he was sixteen, he voiced his troubles to his mother.

She'd noticed that he didn't go and serve at mass every day during the previous summer holidays. Now she understood why. He was caught on the horns of a dilemma.

He believed his latent interest in girls was inherently sinful. She assured Achille that his thoughts were quite normal for a young man of his age. He alone must decide if he thought he could master this very natural urge. In her heart there was understanding, tinged with disappointment. She would talk the matter over with Monsignor Barton when Achille had returned to college.

Achille left St Edmunds College in July 1950, three months short of his seventeenth birthday, not knowing what he wanted to do in life. Finding a job for a year and the prospect of a further two years National Service would give him the breathing space he needed to think about and plan his future but that was not to be.

He took what proved to be an interesting job as an assistant in a research laboratory. Having spent the previous six years almost exclusively in the company of boys, seminarians and priests, he slowly got used to the presence of girls. He worked with Pamela, who was also a laboratory assistant, liked her, found her attractive and was not too embarrassed in her presence as a working colleague. They even started going out together.

Still being staunchly Catholic but very naïve, it seemed the only solution to his problem was marriage. His mother was shocked when he mentioned his wish to marry. He was not yet eighteen. She didn't think he was ready for marriage. He certainly couldn't support a wife and she certainly didn't think Pamela was a suitable choice. Considerable argument followed but, finally, his mother conceded. If he still felt the same when he finished his National Service, she would give her consent.

As he'd been away from home since the age of eleven, being in the Air Force did not come as a shock as it appeared to do with many young men. What did come as a tremendous shock however, was the routine use of swearwords in ordinary conversation. Also the apparent lack of religion among them, the open and crude talk about the pleasures to be derived from girls bodies. There was even a clear case of overt homosexuality within his billet.

A white wedding with nuptial mass joined Achille and Pamela when they made their marriage vows in 1953. In his naivety he had been surprised at how readily a local company had offered him a good job in the accountancy department. He had not realized that, with a Public School education, he was a very marketable young man.

Living with Pamela was more difficult than he had imagined. She could be moody and very stubborn. The sex was an enjoyable antidote. Samuel arrived in 1954, followed by Olivia in 1956. Pamela was not interested in having more children, something they had never discussed, so the problem of contraception reared its head. Pamela, a recent Catholic convert was not in agreement with the Catholic attitude to contraception. They had never discussed it. It became a major stumbling block between them.

Achille threw himself ever more vigorously into his work. At the end of his first year his talents had been recognized. He was unaware that they were treating him as a management trainee. They moved him to the purchasing department for a year then into sales training. Then he was put on the road as a salesman, rising to regional manager within a further year. Finally, having made an all round assessment of him, they put him into marketing as a brand manager. By 1958 it was his employers that had decided on the career best suited to his talents and personality; he never looked back.

He'd made sacrifices to achieve this rate of progress. He paid much more attention to his job than his wife and children. He did not see as much of his children as he should. This was exacerbated by strong differences of opinion on various aspects of their rearing. As a consequence of this turmoil in his life, his faith suffered. He'd started missing mass and ever more rarely said his morning or evening prayers, in fact it got to the point where he didn't think about his faith from one day to the next, concentrating almost exclusively on his job. He'd even fallen into the habit of using contraceptives, rather than have yet another argument with his wife. His job was now number one in his life.

****

Part Two

1962 – 1984

Four

A number of other Nazis had made their own way to Southern America quite independently. Most had arrived with only a moderate money supply, simply pleased to have escaped. The committee members employed some of them within the businesses of which they were now partners. In some cases the committee had offered loans, at nominal interest, to gain a wider loyalty. There was now a cadre of twenty-seven Nazis who had escaped prosecution, living comfortable lives, with a sizeable nest egg salted away in Switzerland.

In 1962 the sixteenth annual meeting of the Post War Finance Committee was in progress. It had, as usual, been very carefully planned. The six members, plus Herman Fritz; the pilot, having been invited to join them, arrived from various locations, both from within and outside Argentina. The meeting was being held in a hotel at Adolfo Alsina airport. The room had been carefully swept for bugs and trusted security personnel were discretely placed to ensure absolute privacy.

The next item on the agenda was the management of their funds. Having dealt with sub-items a) and b), they came to c). The chairman, Heinz Gasser, requested that the treasurer report on what progress had been made on the very frustrating sixteen-year question of obtaining the funds from the still unopened Swiss bank security box?

Wolfgang Mack addressed the meeting. "The committee is aware that we have spent considerable time and money trying to trace the document that went missing towards the end of December 1944. It gives the number of the Swiss bank security box that contains the authorisation documents for a series of accounts and deposits. At this year's value their contents has risen to an estimated seventy-five million dollars.

"You will recall that Bruno Affleck, one of our senior civil servants, stole the document. He admitted this during his painful interrogation but, unfortunately, did not reveal to whom he passed it, before he died. You will also recall, we thought our problem was solved early in '45 when we caught Stephen Simpson, the English spy. He also died at our hands, revealing what he'd been doing during the war but gave no a hint of any involvement with the bank security box number and account list.

"Our investigations have eliminated all our suspects, one by one, until last year, when we were left with the most unlikely of them all - Ulrich Hoffman. He was a cryptographer in the Swiss diplomatic service. He worked in the Swiss Legation in Berlin from September '42 and left, along with all the Swiss staff, at the end of December '44.

"We have established some facts:

- He attended a Catholic Church regularly. We think he could well have met Bruno Affleck who attended the same church there.

- We know that Hoffman started going out with a Maureen Alcock when he was working in the Swiss embassy in England, sometime between April '36 and March '39. She was one of the multi-lingual secretaries working for the English Diplomatic Service.

- Sometimes, the English unmarried secretaries accepted overseas postings. It is possible that Miss Alcock's posting to Switzerland was pre-planned by the British so that Hoffman could pass information to them via her?

- The Swiss were generally true to their neutrality but we suspect that Hoffman was privately involved in some forms of espionage. This we think was arranged when he was in England. His agreement might have been due to his religious beliefs, English sympathies or influenced by his growing attachment to Miss Alcock.

- We think they pretended to meet for the first time at a diplomatic function some time in '42, when Ulrich Hoffman had returned to Switzerland from Spain. She had taken up her overseas posting to their Berne embassy in mid '41. It is clear that their relationship developed beyond co-operation.

- They were obviously in communication, via the diplomatic bag, during his time in Germany but were never suspected of espionage. When he returned to Berne in December '44 the relationship matured. They were in their early 40s when they married in July '45.

- If he was the recipient of the box number and list, he has never capitalised on it. Their married lifestyle and living standard has been what one would expect for a Swiss diplomat in his position. He could have decided that it would court disaster to approach the bank. Neither can we detect a British approach to the bank over the last fifteen years. As they are our last remaining option, we decided to target Mrs Hoffman first. We assumed she would be the softer target from whom to extract the information as she was also in the middle of a secret affair. This, we felt, would add to her vulnerability.

- We entered their home nine weeks ago when Mr. Hoffman was sent to Madrid for a few days and she was with her lover in Basel. We searched the house thoroughly and found nothing relevant. Then we confronted her on her return.

There is no need to go into details about what our people did to her, suffice it to say she ultimately died. She did reveal that they had conducted espionage, mostly related to the VI flying bomb and the VII rocket. They also passed information to the English relating to the first jet fighter, the Me 262A which finally entered service in October '44. We are assured however, that she had no knowledge of our Swiss bank document.

"Our men could not snatch Mr. Hoffman on his return from Madrid from under the noses of the heavy police presence investigating his wife's death. It would have been far too risky. Unfortunately he proved to be extremely alert to the possibility of our existence. He left immediately after her funeral and has disappeared without trace. He drew his savings and disappeared, leaving behind his home, his job, his friends, the police investigation - in fact everything."

Following their discussion, the committee decided to continue to pursue Mr. Hoffman. His timely departure gave them a real belief that at long last they were on the right track.

****

Five

During the party to celebrate their tenth wedding anniversary in 1963, Achille had an intuitive, depressing and unbidden thought that would prove to be a mental watershed in his life. He suddenly realised that he was only thirty and could not face the prospect of another thirty, forty or perhaps even fifty years with Pamela. His marriage vows and the fact that Samuel and Olivia were only nine and seven brought him down to earth. He must persevere, at least for some years to come, for the sake of the children. But now there was a chink in his armour, the damage had been done; a seismic shift in his mental attitude to his marriage had taken place, presaging another major step in the decline of his faith.

There was now an inherent, if sub-conscious disposition that accepted the idea of an affaire. Some two years later he had the first of these with one of the women in the local Conservative Party. Then came a rather exciting affaire with his wife's best friend, enhanced by the potentially explosive outcome, if discovered?

Then in 1967 he fell in love with one of the secretaries at work, Miriam Byfield. As working colleagues, they had known and liked each other for three years. One evening, when he was working late, she had been delayed by her boss and tapped on his window to wave goodbye and impulsively blew him a kiss as she walked to her car. That was the spark between them that lit the fire of an affaire that turned into real love.

Miriam was a divorcee who came to know quite a lot about his life. She had a daughter called Amber who was much the same age as Olivia. Olivia was now the only bright spot at home, the apple of his eye. Whilst he doted on her, his wife thought that Samuel could do no wrong. This was yet another source of argument between Achille and Pamela. The children were now being raised on an almost daily diet of noisy arguments which caused Olivia in particular to rush up to her bedroom, slam her door to try and cut out the noise and then cry herself to sleep time and time again.

One evening in 1968 the dam burst. Achille could take no more. He first went very quiet, then simply walked out of the house to his car and drove off. He later explained how he felt to Miriam but it was clear that his conscience troubled him concerning the children, Olivia's situation in particular.

Samuel was fourteen, old enough to begin to understand and he saw first hand, the devastating effect this abandonment had on his mother. His relationship with his father, which had never been brilliant, was strained. Olivia, who was only twelve, felt totally betrayed by her father whom she loved dearly. Her mother's frustration was taken out on her even more than before, which made her feelings of being let down many times worse.

Achille who, ever conscious of his obligations, continued to make his wife a housekeeping allowance and paid the mortgage on the four-bedroom house. His wife divorced him in 1971 on the grounds of adultery and a little later married Philip. Achille had moved in with Miriam and, after the divorce, he married her in a Registry Office. He also began to visit his children which proved rather difficult at first. Slowly the ice melted and the adults were at least civil to one another.

Olivia started to phone her dad when she was upset, usually from a public call box, on her way to or from school. She occasionally phoned in the evening if she was alone and, when he was away, she began to confide in Miriam. One day in 1972, a few weeks before her sixteenth birthday, she phoned and Miriam could tell she was very more upset than usual.

Slowly the picture of what had happened emerged. Her stepfather Philip had forced her to get undressed, threatening he would tell his wife about her trying to arouse him with her body. They were alone in the house. She knew it was all wrong and very reluctantly she began to undress. She'd got down to her bra and panties, was about to remove them, when her mother came home unexpectedly early. Philip told her to remember his threat and left to go and greet Pamela. Olivia was afraid of what could happen and what he might do to her?

Achille was due back from abroad later that same evening and Miriam had agreed to meet him at the airport. Having a daughter of similar age, she instinctively told Olivia to make some excuse for going out, going to help her friend with her homework or something and she would pick her up. She took Amber with her, explaining that Olivia was very upset, then picked her up at the pre-arranged spot on their way to collect Achille from the airport.

Olivia lived with her father, Miriam and Amber from that day on. Olivia got on well with Amber. She liked Miriam a lot and her father never told her the outcome. He simply sorted out the problem. All she ever knew was that he collected all her things over the next few days and heard no more about it until very much later in life. Suffice to say, the ice that existed between her father and mother got a great deal thicker and did nothing to help her father's strained relationship with his son Samuel.

****

As a result of finding true love and resolving the turmoil in his life, Achille's work improved significantly. A few months later, he was appointed Marketing Manager when that position became vacant. His particular forte proved to be in product development, the interface between marketing and engineering. He soon represented the UK Company in European meetings, even visiting the parent company in the USA.

He was very happy with Miriam and the relationship got

even better when Olivia joined them. She and Amber had birthdays that were only seven weeks apart. The joint celebration of his promotion and their sixteenth birthdays set a wonderful seal on the new family relationship.

****

In '73 Achille had to go to Basel on a Friday. He was used to hiring cars at the various airports. He decided to stay over that night and drive down to Solothurn, just over forty miles to the south on the Saturday morning.

When he got there he managed to park by the Basel gate and visited the tourist information office to obtain a town map. He then had a look round the town centre, stopping briefly for a coffee. Referring to the map, he drove out of the car park turning east on to the Innere Baselstresse, left into Werkhofstrasse and then took a right turn into St. Niklausstrasse. A few hundred metres along that road are two car parks, near the footpath that leads into the woods to the northeast of Solothurn. He walked into the woods and entered a gorge within a few minutes of parking the car.

He'd taken the 1938 photo his mother had given him. He stood by the chapel on the left, the one with the steps and compared the photo with the Hermitage. Little seemed to have changed. The only difference was that now a hermit had added a window box of flowers to the upper window.

Being a Saturday, a few people were strolling by. He tried in vain to remember his 1938 visit and noticed that a hermit was working in the shade, on a little kitchen garden to the right of his home. His face was hidden by a thick beard, a heavy moustache and of course the shade. He strolled back and forth taking-in the details, trying to compare it in his mind's eye to the watercolour on his mother's wall. The hermit noticed how Achille's behaviour differed from the usual visitors. He stopped working and came across to the little fence and caught

Achille's attention.

"I couldn't help noticing you lingering and looking round and also looking at something in your hand," he said.

With some surprise Achille said, "How did you know I spoke English?"

"One gets to distinguish tourists from locals; I just made an informed guess."

"Your English is very good, I must say."

"Thank you. One doesn't get the practice these days. I learnt it at school but worked in England for a while, many years ago."

"I was looking round and comparing what's here with this photo and with a painting my mother has at home. It seems that not much has changed over the years. The only difference I can see is that you, or someone before you, have added a window box at the upper level of your Hermitage," and he handed him the photo.

"Where did you get this?" the hermit asked.

"My mother gave it to me. She comes from Solothurn and brought me here in 1938 when she came to visit her parents. She took it when I crouched down for a drink at that water fountain."

"The mention of water reminds me I could do with a drink. I'm a bit dry from working in the garden. Why don't you come in and we can have a tea or coffee?"

"That's very kind of you - I'd like that." Achille introduced himself by holding out his hand and saying, "My name's Achille Aarden. I'm very pleased to meet you."

"I'm Max Seiber," he said and they shook hands as they walked up the short path.

The hermit's room they entered had two chairs, a scrubbed table, a paraffin lamp, a wood-burning stove on which Max boiled the water for tea but the most notable feature was the books. Achille remarked on this.

"Well, I've got the time; I do a lot of reading. I like to

broaden my mind. Tell me more about your mother?"

"Well, she was born here in Solothurn in 1906. Her maiden name was Bruchner. Her Christian name is Emilia and my father called her Emmy. I think her second name was Anne or Anna. She was the eldest of three. Her two younger sisters were Liddy and Helen. Liddy married and moved to Zurich and Helen became a Benedictine nun, nursing TB patients in a convent sanatorium in Davos. My mother came to England in 1924 to learn English. She met my father, outside church after mass one Sunday. The rest, as they say, is history."

"How interesting, you must have been very young when your mother brought you here. Do you remember it at all?"

"Well I was four and a half. I remember very little. I was born in October '33. I know it must have been Easter time in '38 when we came because my grandparents hid chocolate eggs in the garden for me to find. I also remember some of the train journey, mother settling me down to sleep on the seat beside her. There were only the two of us in the carriage compartment. I don't know if there were any sleepers then or if we just couldn't afford one? I also remember my grandparents had a rocking horse in an outhouse but I find I can't remember anything about my visit here to the gorge."

"At that age I'm surprised you remember that much. What made you decide to come here after all these years?"

"Well I now have to travel quite a lot on business, I happened to be coming to Basel, so I decided to stay-over for a night. My mother promised me her water-coloured Indian ink drawing of this gorge and gave me this photo a few years ago. Mother's in her late sixties now and I thought it would be nice to come here and then surprise her and tell her about my visit when I go to see her next. May I ask what made you decide to become a hermit and live here, I've never met a hermit?"

"Well my wife and I didn't have any children; she got killed some years ago, so I decided to retire early. My observation of the war as a Swiss neutral made me think more deeply about man's brutality to man and the meaning of life. I was born, worked and lived in Berne and this Hermitage is well known. It's only thirty kilometres from the capital. I'd heard it was empty and a life of quiet contemplation appealed to me, so I came here about fifteen years ago."

"What's it like to be a hermit here?"

"Well I'm not an ascetic, I'm just an ordinary man seeking a degree of solitude. Local people are generous. They know I'll pray for them when they leave me basic foods like bread, milk, cheese, tinned foods and candles. One brings me a cooked meal twice a week; I just have to heat it up on the stove. I supplement their gifts with vegetables from my little garden. Other people leave small donations by the water fountain so I can do a bit of shopping with it and the small income from my savings. It also means I can afford to indulge in the luxury of another book from time to time.

"I spend a period each day reading the bible and meditating, do a little gardening as you saw and walk into town two or three times a week for mass."

"I read most of the New Testament when I was younger but not the Old Testament. I found some of it interesting but not absorbing. What is it that appeals to you?"

"Well the Old Testament appeals on a number of different levels really. First it's full of stories, many as good as some of the best novels. Peace and war, good and evil, happiness and misery, murder, battles and family feuds, jealousy and lust, courtship and marriage, betrayal and tyranny, harvests and famine, opulence: There are some really marvellous stories.

"I divide the bible into two - it's either history or forecasts. It's a detailed record of mankind's early life on earth, with the first chapter of Genesis, - the world's pre-history. Talking of Genesis, isn't it amazing, that long before we knew about such things, someone was inspired and wrote down how the world, its fauna and flora, were created. Darwin and others have subsequently proved that the earth evolved in exactly the same sequence as told in Genesis. It surely can't just be a coincidence."

"Do you think the Bible is literally true then?"

"Within the parameters of human error, coloured by memory and context - yes. As I think one of your English professors used to say, I forget his name; 'it depends on what you mean by truth'. The knowledge of those who wrote the Bible was very limited by today's standards. In Genesis, for example, they didn't know about the 'Big Bang' theory of how the universe was created. It's simply God-given inspiration to its scribe.

"When it talks of the Universe being created in six days, the scribe only had the earth's days as a yardstick as a period of time. Einstein had not shown how time is a variable dimension - that it's not an absolute. Nor did astronomy exist to tell them how other planets have differing lengths of day because they spin at differing speeds, or constellations that take thousands of years for just one revolution - all are a 'day' by the same rotational yardstick.

"So many things are possible, even beyond our current understanding. Yes I do believe it's true, within the context of the writer's level of knowledge and memory, as well as his understanding at the time of writing. We're all influenced in what we say, do or write, by our memory, level of knowledge and environment.

"I am going on rather, aren't I! You didn't come here to listen to an old man rambling on, I'm sure."

"No, don't apologise, I asked the question. It's interesting to listen to someone who's had the time to think much more deeply than I have. It has been most interesting to meet and talk with you. My mother will be jealous but I'm going to have to go back to Basel to catch my plane. I only came to have a look at Solothurn and the gorge but it's been a nice bonus to have tea and to chat with you. Thanks for the tea. Perhaps when I'm next in Switzerland I can come and visit you again?"

"Yes, I'd like that but you must stay longer next time so that we can talk at greater length. If you do come, please try to bring your mother's watercolour if she'll let you, I'd like to see it very much."

Achille reflected on his meeting and conversation with Max Seiber on the flight home that Saturday afternoon. He really liked him.

When he was at college the priests were only concerned with the New Testament and Christianity; the Old Testament being about Jewish history.

Achille now shied away from thinking about religion. He'd committed adultery many times, left his wife and broken his marriage vows, then married a divorcee in a Registry Office. He couldn't undo what he'd done. He couldn't turn the clock back and neither did he want to. He was happy at long last but his lack of faith and separation from God nagged at his conscience.

He must go and visit mother soon, to tell her about his visit. He and Pamela had rarely visited her. She'd not approved of Pamela. She was quite right, as it turned out. The constant arguments were not conducive to making a visit. In any event conversation was always stilted and Pamela was always uncomfortable. On the other hand his mother liked Miriam and he'd been very pleasantly surprised when she and all three of his sisters had accepted their invitation to the wedding reception.

****

On the Friday following Achille Aarden's visit, Max Seiber went into town as usual, to go to mass and then to do his bit of shopping. After mass he went for his usual coffee with his old friend, the pastor of St. Ur's, Canon Zimmerman. Over coffee he said he'd had an unusual visitor whose mother, by coincidence, was born in Solothurn.

"It would be nice if we could look-up the baptismal register for 1906, to see if an Emilia Anne or Anna Bruchner, his mother, was listed there," he said. "Although she could have been baptised at another church."

After they'd finished coffee they went and looked. They worked their way through 1906, until they got to November and there it was.

"She had two sisters, Liddy and Helen," said Max, "while we're here, can we look for those as well?"

"Why are you so interested?" asked his friend.

"Well, I'm sure he'll come again. I'd like to be able to tell him we looked them up and found their baptismal entries." There was nothing in '07 but Liddy was listed in '08. It was not until 1911 that Helen was baptised.

"Will you do me a copy of each; I'd like to give them to him when he comes again?"

"But of course, you can pick them up on Sunday, no charge," he said, with a laugh.

Max then went on to say, "Helen's interesting. Apparently she became a Benedictine nun and went to a convent sanatorium, nursing TB patients in Davos. She'd be sixty-two now, perhaps with your contacts you could make enquiries, see if she's still alive. He didn't say any more about her."

It was Gunter Zimmerman who raised the topic of the unusual visitor that had so interested Max, the following Friday, again over coffee.

"I don't know why but during the week I went through the marriage register as well, searching for a Mr. Bruchner, prior to November 1906. I found what must have been the girls' parents in May 1904 - Herman Bruchner and Emilia Biel, here, I've made you a copy of that as well."

"That's good of you Gunter, I hadn't thought of that. Were you able to find out anything about Helen?"

"Oh yes, quite a nice surprise - she entered the convent of St. Vincent, in Davos as a noviciate in 1929 at the age of eighteen and now she's Reverend Mother would you believe?"

"Is she indeed?"

"Apparently, as TB declined, they had a hard time making ends meet. She persuaded the Mother Superior and the Bishop, to allow them to take in bed, breakfast and evening meal 'back packers', as hotels in Davos are far too expensive for the youngsters."

"Well I never, she a Reverend Mother and running a 'hotel'. I thought there was something special, something different about him; his name's Achille Aarden by the way, that special something must run in the family.

"Thanks for doing that Gunter - I really appreciate it. When he comes again and if he's here over a weekend, I'll introduce you. I'm sure he'll be pleased that we followed up on his visit and you can then tell me what you think."

****

Achille visited his mother about two weeks after his trip to Basel and the visit to the gorge. Olivia, who was now eighteen, had seen very little of her paternal grandma and asked to go with him. She'd just finished her A-levels and was waiting to go on a British Airways stewardess-training course.

Mother was pleased to see them and even more pleased that Olivia had chosen to come. As they drank tea, Achille told his mother all about his visit to Solothurn and his meeting with the hermit. That he'd taken the trouble to go there gave her great pleasure and his story brought tears to her eyes. She questioned him on what Solothurn was like now. She hadn't been there for very many years. She used to go to Switzerland regularly for her holidays and invariably stayed with her sister Helen, at the convent in Davos.

She went and fetched the water-coloured, Indian-ink

picture saying he could now keep it, not just borrow it, as he'd asked. She knew he had a real interest in Switzerland, Solothurn and the Verena Gorge.

When they'd left and were on the drive home, Olivia had the picture on her lap. She noticed along the bottom was written, Solothurn - Eremitage - Soleure, it also had an envelope stuck on the back and she said, "Tell me something about this picture dad, please."

"Well there's a lot of history attached to it. There's some Swiss family history, which you'll probably find interesting now you've grown up and some Swiss history. Your Grandma was actually born in Solothurn you know."

"I didn't know. Her English is so good you can't tell she was Swiss. I always thought we came from Belgium, our surname Aarden is Belgian isn't it?"

"Yes, my paternal grandparents, your great, great grandparents came from there. They were refugees in the First World War. They came from a village called Loppem, just outside Brugge. Their names were Achille and Emma, now you know where those names came from. My father was the eldest. He died when I was fourteen. Then came Pascal, William and Romany. She went back to Belgium to become a nun and to teach in a girl's convent school in a place called Izagem."

"Then how come your father married a Swiss lady?"

"Well, your Grandma came to England to learn English when she was eighteen in 1924. Her maiden name was Bruchner. She stayed with her great aunt and uncle. They were already here. He was the managing director of an Anglo-Swiss firm. She and my father met one Sunday after mass, outside church. They married and had your aunts Emma, Anna and after I came along, your Aunt Eileen.

"Mother took me to Switzerland in 1938 when I was four and a half. She went to visit her parents and her two sisters, my aunt Liddy and Aunt Helen. Helen also became a nun, nursing patients in a T B sanatorium in Davos.

"When we were in Solothurn, mother took me for a walk to the Verena Gorge, in woods on the north-eastern edge of the town. She took a photo of me drinking from the water fountain there; You'll find a print in the envelope on the back."

"So that's you, by the little cross, when you weren't quite five. It's almost the same as in the painting dad?"

"Yes, that's right Olivia, my very first visit to the Verena Gorge. A nice old hermit lived there then and came out of the house to see us. Mother stayed to have a chat with him but I couldn't understand a word. If you look at the watercolour, the hermitage in the photo is on the right, the other two buildings, not in the photo, are small chapels. The hermitage in the painting hasn't got the extension that's in the photo, so it must have been done some time before 1938. So this watercolour's getting on for a hundred years old!"

"It's clear that Eremitage means hermitage in English, at the bottom of the picture but why Soleure as well as Solothurn?"

"Well maybe the painter should have added 'Soletta' as well, because Switzerland uses three main languages - German, French and Italian. However, the majority of Swiss speak Schwyzertutsch, a form of Swiss-German."

"The Swiss family connection is new to me and we learnt very little at school about it, just where it is in Europe and the fact that it's neutral, so tell me more about it?"

"Well Switzerland is made up of twenty-three areas called cantons, rather like English counties. It became Confederation Helvetica in 1650, later known as Switzerland. Its neutrality was declared at the Congress of Vienna in 1815.

"Berne is the capital and Solothurn City is just 19 miles north. It's called a city because the church of St. Ursen and St. Victor is one of the finest Baroque cathedrals in Europe but it's quite a small town really. The Romans originally named it Salodurum. It became a free city of the Holy Roman Empire in

1218.

"Sixty-six men of a Roman legion, led by St. Ursen and St. Victor, had become Catholic. They escaped to Salodurum to avoid execution by Emperor Maximilian. They were eventually caught and beheaded for their faith.

"A young lady called Verena followed the legion all the way from Rome, out of her love and affection for Victor. She ministered to the sick with herbal remedies until she was arrested. She also refused to worship Roman gods but her captor - Hirtakus, became ill. She succeeded in curing him where all the doctors had failed. She was rewarded by being released and allowed to return to her cave in what is now called the Verena Gorge. Hermits have lived in the gorge, on-and-off, ever since; I really liked the one I met a couple of weeks ago."

****

Six

It was about nine months later when Achille visited Max for the second time. He had to go to Geneva, to an innovation exhibition. He arranged to be there on the Friday to give him the weekend in Switzerland. It's about a hundred and twenty mile drive to Solothurn from there so, as he was tired from a busy day, he decided to stay over and drive there on the Saturday morning.

It's a fairly straightforward drive. The E4 was, by that time, almost all motorway and it runs virtually 'door-to-door'. He arrived at the Ambassador hotel in Solothurn, in time for an early lunch. It's on the opposite side of the river from the town centre. He walked to the gorge after lunch for the exercise. It took less than half an hour and he even remembered to take the watercolour with him.

Max was surprised to see him back so soon and seemed genuinely pleased. He was making a cup of coffee after his own lunch, so they both had one. They talked about why Achille had come to Switzerland again, about his drive from Geneva, the quality of the exhibition and what his mother had to say about his earlier visit and, of course, he was pleased to show him the picture.

Max thought it was very pretty if somewhat idealised. The cliff faces of the gorge cut out more light, which made it somewhat duller. He also remarked on the lack of an extension to what was now his home. "We get artists painting here occasionally," he said, "but this is certainly one of the better ones I've seen. Thanks for taking the trouble to bring it. It's so nice to see what it was like so many years ago."

He then told Achille that he and his friend - Canon Zimmerman - had looked-up the baptismal register at St. Ur's. They'd found his mother's entry and those of her two sisters. He surprised Achille by telling him that they'd also found his grandparents wedding recorded there. Their names were Herman and Anna Bruchner. Then, pulling some papers from a shelf, he handed them to Achille, I asked the Canon to make copies for you."

"I don't know what to say but thanks. My mother will be delighted to see them I'm sure," he said.

Achille then harked back to their conversation of nine months earlier, by saying, "When I was here before, you said that the horrors of war made you want to think more deeply about life. As Switzerland is neutral I wondered why it had affected you so deeply? I didn't understand what was going on during the war myself; I was a small schoolboy when it started."

"Well, when I told you I worked in Berne, that wasn't strictly true, I worked in the Swiss Diplomatic Service and was posted abroad from time to time. I was born a couple of years before your mother, in 1904. At school I found I had a gift for languages, I lived with my parents in Berne and read politics at university. My father was a civil servant.

"Berne being the capital, the diplomatic service seemed the right place for me. My first exposure to war, like you, was as a somewhat older schoolboy over twenty years earlier, during the First World War. I joined the Diplomatic Service ten years after that war ended, when I'd finished at university in 1928.

"I started as a translator but political events in Germany, after President Hindenburg was persuaded to make Hitler the Chancellor in January 1933, made me change my mind. As you can imagine, it became the main topic of conversation in the diplomatic service. The events that unfolded pushed Germany to the top of the diplomatic agenda, as the Nazi party's true colours became progressively clearer.

"In February 1933, thirty-three Decrees were published, which included the banning of rival political meetings or publications. Then came the dissolution of the Prussian parliament and raids on the Communist Party offices. An arsonist fire in the Reichstag caused Hitler to be given emergency powers by Presidential Decree and that was just February!

"Many nasty and evil events are indelibly printed on my mind. I was still only twenty-nine and having studied politics I was both fascinated and horrified by what was happening. The talk in the Service was all about where this would lead? March saw the rounding-up of thousands of dissenting Germans who were put into camps; the infamous Dachau concentration camp was opened then. In March *Ermachtigungsgesetz* was passed, sorry, that's an Enabling Law, which gave Hitler special powers for four years. An unstoppable momentum was gathering pace. Where would it end?

"In April came an official boycott of Jewish shops and Jewish professional men, showing that the views expressed by Hitler in *Mein Kampf* were now being turned into a reality. In May the Labour Unions were dissolved and in June a law was passed that made it an offence for anyone to betray the German economy.

"You can imagine, Achille, that for someone who was a practising Catholic who'd studied politics and was relatively new to the diplomatic service, it was an emotionally moving time. Our neutrality frustrated me. I felt I wanted to play a more active role and applied for a move. Of course at that time one didn't know the depth of the horrors that were to be perpetrated by that regime."

"Yes, I think I can understand your feelings. It must have been a difficult time. I was only born in October '33, so all these events, which started before I was born, are fascinating, please tell me more."

"In the October, the month of your birth, all journalists in Germany had to be registered and licensed. In November came the first outspoken criticism, Cardinal Faulhaber had the courage to call the Nazis anti-Christian.

"It was June of the following year, 1934, that a shot was fired at Hitler, an attempted assassination. In fact it wounded Himmler, the head of the Gestapo. Hundreds were taken to Licherfelde and shot, including the ex-Chancellor von Schleicher. In July, Eicke shot Rohm in his prison cell and a retrospective law was issued legitimising all the killings. Matters were becoming very serious. There was deep concern in the diplomatic world.

"In August President Hindenburg died. The office of President was abolished and Hitler became supreme. There was no one left to challenge his authority. In March of '35 Hitler renounced the disarmament clauses of the Treaty of Versailles. In April the existence of the Luftwaffe was announced and in September the Nazi swastika was made the national flag. It was then that we in the diplomatic service realised that events in Germany were beginning to shape up for another war. With Hitler having so much power, would Swiss neutrality also become threatened?

"My departmental transfer came through in November '35, I had to report for training on January 1st '36. Germany decreed, in that month, that being an Aryan was now a precondition of any public appointment - another blow against the Jews.

"My training ended in March '36 and I got my first posting overseas to England, in the April. I settled into my new role and rented a flat in Brook Green in West London, fairly near Hammersmith. I then began to see things from a slightly different perspective, coloured by the English Diplomatic Service and the BBC news.

"It was a year later, in April 1937, during the Spanish Civil War that one of the most shocking events occurred, German planes carpet-bombed civilians in Guernica. It shook the world, not only was this the first time a town had ever been carpet-bombed, it was only the second time non-combatants had been directly targeted in war. The first was on England by

46

German Zeppelins in 1916.

"In 1938 the pace of events quickened. In January the Commander-in-Chief of the army was forced to resign on false charges of homosexuality. This allowed Hitler to add to his power in February, by becoming Minister of War and Commander-in-Chief of the armed forces. The bully in Hitler spread abroad; he started to throw his weight about. The Austrian Chancellor was given an ultimatum, which led to *Anschluss* in March - Austria effectively became part of Germany, without a fight.

"Hitler brought the Condor Legion back from Spain in May and the English Prime Minister visited Hitler in July to consult with him on Czechoslovakia. He went to see Hitler again, with Mussolini in September when they agreed that the Sudetenland should go to Germany. Then in October Germany occupied parts of Czechoslovakia.

"In November came *'Crystal Nacht'*, when more than 20,000 Jews were imprisoned; decrees eliminated Jews from the economy and their children were expelled from school. Finally, in December, all Jewish shops and firms were handed over to Aryans.

"March '39 was the end of my three-year assignment in England and I returned to Switzerland. Then, after detailed briefing I was sent to Spain and witnessed the aftermath of the Civil War. I saw the most dreadful retribution.

"In that same month Germany occupied Bohemia and Moravia on the pretence of being their protectors. In August they signed a Soviet-German non-aggression pact. An Anglo-Polish treaty of mutual assistance, countered this. However, in September Germany invaded Poland causing Britain and France to declare war. The Soviet Union also invaded Poland, ostensibly to ensure the integrity of its own borders. But, during October, Poland was virtually overrun.

"Germany invaded Denmark and Norway in April 1940 then the Netherlands, Belgium, Luxemburg and France in May.

You perhaps recall mention of the Dunkirk evacuation of the English expeditionary force? Being a boy, you were no doubt aware of aircraft, the bombing and the Battle of Britain, the introduction of rationing and so on?"

"I don't remember a great deal, I was only seven when it started but I learnt a lot about the war after it ended."

"I was thankful to be recalled from Spain in December '41. I was pleased to have some time in Switzerland, then I was thrown into the thick of things by being posted to Berlin in September '42. This was the time I had first-hand exposure to the horrors of war. The inhumanity of man to man - one did not have to look far to see the egos of the higher ranks running roughshod over ordinary German men and women. Their belief in the Third Reich and the building of an empire to last a thousand years was absolute.

"They forgot about God. They were gods. They were invincible. They indulged in every kind of perversity, breaking all His Commandments in the pursuit of pleasure - live for today. They were proud, lustful; avariciously taking prized possessions, in fact repeatedly committing most, if not all of the seven deadly sins. It was disgraceful. The events during my time in Germany, is really why I'm here today.

"The success of the Anglo-American landings in Normandy marked the beginning of the end. Our government finally decided to recall us at the end of December '44, as the war was nearing its conclusion.

"I had a shock on the second Sunday of that December as I walked down the aisle after mass. A member of the congregation, who was a nodding acquaintance, quickly pushed a paper into my pocket without acknowledging me or saying a word. We had spoken only occasionally after mass, I knew him to be a senior civil servant in the German administration. He knew I was a Swiss diplomat. My impression had been that he equally disliked the behaviour exhibited by many of the German hierarchy.

"When I got back to my apartment, I took the paper out of my pocket to have a look. It was a list of letters and numbers. I had the impression that the first was probably a Swiss bank's security box number, the rest were possibly bank account numbers but I wasn't sure? I realised his need to get rid of the list surreptitiously spelt potential danger for me. We were due to leave in just over two weeks, so I decided to keep it hidden in case he contacted me before then.

"Unfortunately, ten days later he was found murdered; I then became very frightened indeed. Thoughts raced through my mind, I had six days to survive before we all left Switzerland. Was it the key to someone's ill-gotten gains? Possibly. Was he murdered because of the document? Probably. Did anyone see him put the paper in my pocket? Maybe. Was I now, therefore, a target? Could be. He hadn't told me what to do with it and now he was dead; I wondered what on earth I should do?

"I decided to play safe. I transferred the letters and numbers onto some of my own papers. I split them up and in so doing I encoded them but in such a way that I could re-assemble them if need be. Then I burnt the original. I waited in fear for six days and nights, thinking that the Gestapo might come for that sheet of paper. It might be in the day when I was out; they could ransack my apartment to find it. If I was a suspect I might be tortured but, at least, I could honestly deny its existence. Thankfully in the event nothing happened, I was extremely relieved at our return to 'sanity' in Switzerland.

"The journey home was constantly interrupted by damaged transport links. The clearance by and through the German border at Basel, was unbearable. It was when I got back home and the pressure was off that I realised just how stressful the two and a quarter years in Berlin had been and those last two weeks in particular. Although we had diplomatic status, we were not immune from suspicion or surveillance. We had broken sleep most nights, spending them in the basement

49

below the embassy because of the constant bombing.

"Latterly we had been dealing with a very greatly stressed German hierarchy that had become increasingly frenetic as the tide of the war turned against them. We suffered deteriorating food supplies, deteriorating communications and a progressive lack of real purpose. My last six days there were the very worst I've ever experienced; the relief of being in Berne once again was unimaginably wonderful.

"As a matter of interest, the Swiss legation was located in a really lovely building: We'd been there since 1920. I later learned that the skeleton staff that remained, who were local German employees, were arrested by the Russians when they occupied Berlin and were taken to Russia. The Red Army had decided to use our building as their Headquarters in Berlin."

Achille agreed to meet Max at St Ur's for the ten o'clock mass on the Sunday morning. Achille had not been to mass for almost fifteen years and was surprised it was in German and not Latin. He later learned that much had changed in the Catholic Church since the Second Vatican Council of '62 -'65. The Pastoral Constitution's change to the vernacular language was implemented across the world during 1971.

After mass, Max took Achille to meet his friend Canon Zimmerman for coffee, as promised. The small talk led Canon Zimmerman to say he understood from Max that Achille had an aunt who was a nun in Davos and asked if he ever visited her? Achille told him he'd been there two years ago with his wife and went on to explain.

"I'd had a Thursday meeting at our factory in Lecco and my wife had come with me. That evening I took her to La Scala, where I'd booked a box for a concert. The following morning we left the Grisso hotel in Lecco to drive to Davos. We had a beautiful journey alongside Lake Como to Chiavenna, then up through St.Moritz, on to Zernez, then over the Fluelapass to Davos."

Achille told them that Aunt Helen was Reverend Mother for the third or fourth time. He explained they could only hold the role for three years, then they had to stand down for at least one year, under the rules of the order. "She couldn't speak English, so we had planned the visit whilst my mother was there on holiday.

"We had a lovely two days 'exploring' Davos. I was impressed with the old *Rathouse* - particularly the local council chamber with its huge tiled wood-burning stove. We left on the Sunday afternoon to drive down through Klosters and Landquart to pick up the N13 and N3 motorways to Zurich and caught our plane home."

Achille remembered to thank Max and Gunter for thinking to study the baptismal register at St. Ursen's and make copies. "I was very pleased. I'm sure mother will be too, I'd forgotten my grandparent's names."

Achille told them that he learnt quite recently, that his real grandfather had died and grandma had re-married before his visit in '38.

As they walked back to the *Eremitage* after their coffee, Achille remarked on Max's frightening time in Germany during the war. He said, "Like a lot of people, I wonder how God allows such evil as the systematic extermination of Jews. On top of which there are thousands, if not millions of deaths from natural disasters such as earthquakes, volcanoes and floods. One of God's commandments is, 'Thou shall not kill' but He seems to have made an imperfect world that does just that - kills?"

"That's a deep question," Max replied, "one I've spent many hours meditating upon over the years. My considered answer is quite involved so why don't you share my lunch. I wasn't expecting you this weekend but I'm sure the cooked lunch I was given to heat, can stretch to the two of us, if we add bread and cheese - what do you think?"

"I've got plenty of time Max; I booked to fly home from Basel to save driving back to Geneva, so I don't need to leave until around four. It's very kind of you to offer me lunch; I'd really enjoy sharing with you and listening to your answer."

Max addressed my question over lunch. "Yes, the holocaust was dreadful but God did warn the Jews. One of the psalms reads, *'Listen, my people, to my warning; how I wish you would listen to me'*. He also said, via the prophet Hosea, *'The God I serve will reject His people, because they have not listened to Him. They will become wanderers among the nations. I will attack this sinful people and punish them. Nations will join together against them'*.

"However, the more deeply I thought about your more fundamental question Achille, the more I realised one should consider why God made the universe the way it is. So I began to meditate on a few references in the bible that might apply. I then began to imagine an event that occurred before time began; my mind moved away from my surroundings into a far more glorious place.

"The Spirit took control of me. There in heaven was a throne with someone sitting on it. His face gleamed like such precious stones as jasper and carnelian and all round the throne there was a rainbow the colour of emerald. In a circle round the throne were twenty-four other thrones, on which were seated twenty-four elders, the seraphim, dressed in white and wearing crowns of gold. From the throne came flashes of lightning, rumblings and peals of thunder. In front of the throne seven lighted torches were burning, which are the seven spirits of God. Also in front of the throne there was what looked like a sea of glass, clear as crystal.

"In rows, stretching back way beyond the seraphim, almost as far as the eye could see, were ranked, cherubim, thrones, dominions, virtues, powers, princedoms, archangels and angels, all dressed in white - it was a truly regal gathering.

"The great king seated on the throne was no ordinary king,

a sight that filled me with awe and wonder. I realised that the multitude were singing of their king's greatness - paying homage to his omnipotence.

"In one small part of this throng I noticed a disturbance. I knew, as if by clairvoyance, that a group, led by one of the princes, was exceedingly jealous of the king's great power. He'd been spreading discord among a host of archangels and angels; these were the rumblings that I'd heard.

"There was no trial, simply immediate autocratic decisiveness. The rebel leader's attire turned black - the garments of his followers likewise. The great king spoke to them in a booming voice of great anger that sounded like the peals of thunder that I'd heard.

"'Be banished forever to the farthest place. There is a deep pit lying between us so that those who want to cross over from here to you cannot do so, nor can anyone cross over to us from where you are. The king's anger and fury was truly awesome. Those who had rebelled were ejected, as Jesus said when he came on Earth - 'I saw Satan fall like lightning from heaven' - and they were gone. The king then spoke to the rest of the assembly in a voice now devoid of anger.

"'I will replace the fallen with new loyal beings who will not rebel - those who come will have earned their place with me. Those that do not will forever join the rebels without ever setting foot in my kingdom.'

"It was at that moment, I think, that God decided to create the Universe and mankind. It was the works of Charles Kingsley that presaged that insight for me. He outlined what I think could have been in God's mind when He created the world.

"Kingsley was an English rector in a parish in Hampshire. He was a highly educated and brilliant social novelist who wrote in the mid to late 1800s. His ideas are the best explanation of this world I've come across, so I adopted them.

"I'll attempt to summarise what Kingsley said. God could have chosen to produce a perfect world but He produced something cleverer - an evolving universe. By bringing into being a creation in which stars, planets and creatures could evolve. This kind of world is extremely clever, because it presents people with the opportunity to earn a place with God in heaven but it has a necessary cost.

"Death is an inevitable part of this evolving universe, be they stars, planets or people, each generation has to give way to the next. In it, genetic mutations are necessary to generate new forms of life but such mutations can also cause malignancy, so such lives can range from good to bad.

"This kind of creation allows terrible events to occur. Not because God is callous or incompetent but because a creation in which stars, planets and creatures make themselves, is necessarily a world of change, ragged edges, blind alleys, a world of transience and death. It makes us reflect on such events, to recognise the power of God and it offers us a challenge. The opportunity for acts of good or evil, to love or hate, to help or harm one another.

"I really think Kingsley has it right, because God said, through Isaiah, *I form the light and create the dark. I make good fortune and create calamity; it is I, the Lord, who do all this.*

"But this world of ours is not the final expression of God's intentions. God's ultimate purpose is that people should be free to choose whether to enter into and embrace a life with God, or not. This second step, to enter another form of life with God, after death, is God's final purpose. God showed us how this can happen through Christ's own life and death, followed by the Resurrection. We are offered his greatest gift, to share in a wonderful new life with him, if we so choose?

"During His Last Supper he knew what His future role would be. He told his apostles, "*There are many rooms in my father's house and I am going to prepare a place for you. I would not tell you this if it were not so. And after I go and prepare a place for you, I will come back and take you to myself, so that you will be where I am. You know the way to the place I am going".*

Thomas said to him, "Lord, we do not know where you are going, so how can we know the way to get there?"

Jesus answered him, "I am the way, the truth and the life; no one goes to the father except through me.

"When He was dying on the cross, He took the opportunity to illustrate what He meant by what he said. One of the two criminals crucified with him said to the other *"Don't you fear God? You received the same sentence He did. Ours however, is only right, because we are getting what we deserve for what we did; but He has done no wrong." And he said to Jesus, "Remember me, Jesus, when you come as king!" Jesus said to him, "I promise you that today you will be in Paradise with me.* Jesus knew he was the one who would decide the fate of each one of us.

"Daniel, during the period of Persian rule, sometime between 550 BC and 400 BC, had a vision:

During this vision in the night, I saw what looked like a human being. He was approaching me, surrounded by clouds and went to the one who had been living forever and was presented to him.

He was given authority, honour and royal power, so that people of all nations, races and languages would serve him. His authority would last forever and his kingdom would never end.

"This vision of Daniel's is reflected in the account given in the Acts of the Apostles where Jesus' ascends to heaven in a cloud.

After saying this, he was taken up to heaven as they watched Him and a cloud hid Him from their sight."

As Achille listened to Max, his words had great resonance within his mind. Now he could understand God's plan more clearly. Max had exposed him to his idea of God's reasoning, His decision to create the Universe, the World, mankind and perhaps much more importantly, why He did it, to offer a place to mankind in heaven.

It was getting close to the time that Achille needed to leave for the drive to Basel. He thanked Max for answering his question so fully and for the lunch. "You've exposed my mind to a whole new area of thought and understanding. Kingsley must have been a most interesting character. You've whetted my appetite, I'll buy and read one or more of his books when I get back. I hope I'll also pay more attention to what is meant by what is written when I next read the bible, not just the story but its meaning."

On the flight home Achille reflected more deeply on the things Max had said. He realised that his young faith was based on learning and practicing his religion by rote. His preoccupation with young women had perhaps caused him to marry far too early. The pressures of that marriage and fatherhood had probably not allowed him the time for his faith to mature.

From Max he had glimpsed a picture of faith, moved by conviction and a sense of purpose. He had made his choice; he could not turn the clock back and undo what he had done. He was happy with Miriam, the two girls and his job. He would continue on his chosen course and let the matter mature in his mind. He would no doubt see Max again and maybe an opportunity to resolve the issue would emerge?

****

After Achille had left, Max took down his bible so that he could check the references of the passages he'd used when talking to him. He also took a new sheet of paper, then sat and listed the biblical quotes he'd used.

The first he found in psalm 81,verse 8 but he wrote

77:81:8.

The second was from the prophet Hosea chapter 9 verse 17 and chapter 10 verse 10 but again he encoded it to read 467: 9: 17 & 10: 10. Then came the book of Revelation, chapter 4 verses 2 to 6 but what he wrote was 738: 4: 2 - 6.

The next quotation was from St. Luke's gospel, chapter 10 and verse 18. This read 55: 10: 18.

The fifth quotation read 55: 16: 26.

The sixth was not a biblical quotation but had come to him at the time of his 'vision', so there was no biblical reference, so he just quoted it in full:

"I will replace the fallen with new loyal beings who will not rebel - those who come will have earned their place with me. Those that do not will forever join the rebels without ever setting foot in my kingdom".

The next was from Isaiah, chapter 45, verse 7, which read 47: 45: 7.

He then turned to St. John's gospel and wrote, 56:14: 2 - 6. Then 55: 23: 40 - 43. Then from the book of Daniel he wrote, 326: 7: 13 - 14 and finally, 2287: 1: 9.

On this occasion he was using a simple telephone dial code, i.e. ABC = 2, DEF = 3 etc.

He then wrote Achille's full name, followed by Maidenhead, England and the date at the bottom of the sheet and filed it with a few similar papers in a plain loose-leaf folder.

****

Seven

It was about twelve months before Achille had to go to Switzerland again on a Friday. He and one of his colleagues had to go to a company in Friedrichshafen for exploratory discussions. It was in southern Germany, on the northern shore of the Bodensee. The nearest airport is Zurich; about a forty-mile drive to Romanshorn on the southern shore with a six-mile ferry crossing to Friedrichshafen.

They went on the Thursday afternoon, had their discussions with the company on the Friday and then drove back to Zurich. Achille dropped his colleague off at Kloten airport, kept the hire car and booked into an airport hotel for the night.

It's a little over fifty-five miles to Solothurn from there and he arrived soon after eleven the following morning, thinking to return Max's hospitality and take him out for lunch. When he got to the *Eremitage* however, Max was nowhere to be found? It was a Saturday and Max would normally be there. When he looked through the window, the place seemed a bit of a mess; it was most unlike Max. Achille got a strong feeling that something had happened to him.

He decided to go and see if Canon Zimmerman was home so he drove back into Solothurn. Luckily he was busy preparing his Sunday homily in time for the Sunday eve mass that evening.

When Gunter answered the ring at the door, Achille said, "Hello Canon, I called at the hermitage. I was going to take Max to lunch but he wasn't there, I wondered if you know where he is?"

Gunter invited him in and they went to his study where he'd been working. After Achille was seated, Gunter told him that Max had been murdered three weeks before. He didn't know how to contact Achille so simply had to wait until he turned up.

Canon Zimmerman had buried him on the previous Wednesday after the police released his body.

Achille was glad he was sitting down. He was stunned and said, "I thought he might be ill in hospital. Death, let alone murder, never entered my head; he was always too alive to think he'd die any time soon."

"Yes" Gunter said "would you like a coffee or something a bit stronger?"

"Coffee would be fine," answered Achille, so Gunter called his housekeeper and asked her to make them some.

"Whilst they waited, Gunter told Achille, "The police are conducting an investigation. Obviously Max's murder begs the question of who and why? Who would want to kill a harmless hermit? The whole of Solothurn is shocked. As far as I know, none of our hermits has ever been murdered in the eight hundred years since they've been living in the gorge."

"I'm shocked as well; I don't know what to say? I'd only met him twice but I already thought of him as a wise friend. I was really looking forward to seeing him again. I must go and visit his grave when I leave."

Gunter's housekeeper brought in the coffee. He asked her if she could stretch lunch for the two of them, saying, "I'm sure Achille would enjoy your cooking; you'd like to join me wouldn't you?".

"Yes, that's very kind of you, if its not too much trouble?" She smiled and said she was sure she could manage to do something and they thanked her.

Gunter continued. "Yes, Max was a good man. I'd known him for a number of years, he read a great deal. We often had quite deep philosophical discussions. He had time to think things through and reach considered and, very often, most interesting opinions.

"I'm glad you thought to come and see me because, coincidentally, about two months ago, I had quite a strange visit from him. He seemed to want to prepare for his passing.

59

He gave me a signed sheet of paper to confirm that in the event of his death, I could have all his possessions, those that I wanted anyway. He also gave me a parcel, saying, 'I'd like you to keep this for Achille Aarden but only give it to him when I'm gone'. I joked about it, saying, 'and what makes you think I'll last longer than you?' I've got it here". He got up and reached to an upper shelf of his bookcase. He passed over a neat, light, A4 sized package.

"He didn't explain himself, I assumed that being seventy-one or two, he'd decided it was time to put his affairs in order."

"What have the police had to say about it?" Achille asked as they started lunch.

"They came to ask if I could throw any light on the matter. A few of my parishioners are in the police force, they knew we were friends. They told me that he'd been stabbed, apparently a knife just below the ribs and up into the heart. Whoever did it had searched the place, heaven knows what for. In fact, the place was a bit of a mess. They asked me if I knew anything: silly questions like 'did he have any enemies?'

"They told me he was something of a mystery man. They were having great difficulty tracing his background and any of his relatives. They'd drawn a blank so far. Apparently there's no local record of our Max Seiber. Yes there are some Seibers but none are relatives of his, so far as they can trace. This is true in both Solothurn and in Berne. They're now doing a countrywide search."

"How long is it since they came to see you?"

"It must be at least two weeks, possibly a bit more."

"After lunch, when I've been to say a prayer at his grave, I think I'll go on to the police station and see if anything else has transpired before I head back to the airport. That is, if they'll tell me."

"Oh, I think they will, they'll probably want to ask you some questions as well, because I told them he sometimes spoke to visitors."

Achille thanked Günter and the housekeeper for lunch and walked into the cemetery and found the fresh grave. He then walked the short distance to the Basel gate and along Innere Baselstrasse to the police station which is on the corner where it joins Werkhofstrasse; it was only a few hundred metres.

Achille was always surprised that wherever he went in the world, except for Japan, he always found that most people spoke at least some English and most spoke it well. The inspector Achille finally met, named Lutzi, was no exception; he was from the south of Switzerland, Bellinzona Achille thought he said, the Italian speaking part anyway.

Achille told him who he was, where he came from, why he'd come to see Max and that Canon Zimmerman had told him he'd been murdered. Inspector Lutzi said, "His home had been virtually ransacked. He lived simply, had very little money; in fact it's all a bit of a mystery at present.

"The only thing we do know is that he's lived in the gorge for fifteen or sixteen years. The biggest mystery is that we haven't been able to trace this particular Max Seiber in the records in Solothurn, Berne, or even across the country. Yes, there are plenty of Seibers but none are relatives so far as we can discover. Max Seiber is certainly a mystery man."

Achille said, "I'm surprised, I thought he would be easy to trace, since he'd been in the Swiss Diplomatic Service until he decided on early retirement after his wife was killed."

"Now, Mr. Aarden, that's real news to me", said Inspector Lutzi, getting quite excited. "How strange, you a casual visitor have probably given me the breakthrough I've been waiting for. You're the first person I've talked to who knew anything about his past, including Canon Zimmerman! Did Max Seiber tell you any more?"

"Yes a little, I didn't get the impression it was a secret though. I seem to remember he was born in Berne in 1904, I know it was close to my mother's birthday. She was born in '06. He said he studied politics in Berne and entered the

Diplomatic Service in the late 20s, certainly well before the Second World War. He was initially a translator but he changed roles within the Service before the war. He didn't say what he did then. I do know that he did a tour of duty in England before the war, then in Spain just after the Civil War and was posted to Germany during World War II but I don't know where he served after that."

"Well at last I've got something I can work on. I can't understand why he never told anyone else but you about his past. I think he might have had a secret past that he wanted to stay that way but then why tell you? But now I can begin to find out, I hope, thanks to you."

"I'm glad I've been of some help. I can't think why I'm the only one he's told? Perhaps you'd be kind enough to let me know what it's all about, once you've unravelled the mystery?"

"Yes, of course I will - I'll probably have more questions for you anyway. Do you have a card?"

"Yes", he said, getting out his wallet. "It's my business card, I'll just write my home address and 'phone number on the back... .. There you are."

"Thank you for coming to see me Mr. Aarden. What you've told me is very interesting. Let's hope it unlocks the door to what's happened. I'll be in touch."

When Achille was waiting at Kloten for his 'plane to London, he took the parcel Gunter had given him from his briefcase and opened it. It contained an A4 loose-leaf folder, with only half a dozen hand written pages, the first of which was a short letter:

Dear Achille,

When you receive this folder I will have passed away. I want you to have it as it contains some of life's secrets.

I don't think I told you that I trained as a cryptographer when I changed jobs in the Diplomatic Service, so forgive the simple codes. I thought you'd enjoy a small challenge; I'm sure you won't have too much difficulty.

God bless you and please pray for me.

Max

At that point Achille's flight was called, so it wasn't until the 'plane had taken off that he turned to the folder once again. When he opened it and saw the first page, he saw what Max meant, it was a list of numbers and letters but it had a person's name, town, country and date at the bottom.

There were only five pages in all and, as he thumbed through them, he came to one bearing his own name, town and country. But the date seemed wrong? He'd have to check in his previous year's diary?

His page had ten entries, the sixth entry had no numbers or letters, it was simply a biblical quotation, he assumed. He skipped the first five entries, as they meant nothing to him at that moment and read the sixth.

"I will replace the fallen with new loyal beings who will not rebel - those who come will have earned their place with me. Those that do not will forever join the rebels without ever setting foot in my kingdom".

He explored his mind to see where it might be in the bible. It didn't seem to fit with either his rudimentary knowledge of the prophets, nor any of the words of Christ when he came on Earth so far as he could remember.

Then slowly a very different memory emerged. Max had answered his question of a year ago, 'Why did God make the world the way it is?' During Max's answer Achille felt sure he'd used these or very similar words.

As he wracked his brains in an attempt to recall all that Max had said, more memories slowly returned. One of the things he remembered was being a bit surprised when he spoke as if he were in a trance. They were walking back to the hermitage after Sunday coffee with the Canon or, perhaps, they were having lunch in the hermitage, he wasn't sure?

It was something like 'the spirit took hold of him - then seeing a face like an emerald, the face of a king'. The more he thought about it, the more he realised that Max must have used a biblical passage, because it sounded like it might be something from the book of Revelation, the last book in the New Testament. He thought this because he recalled that St. John frequently used words such as *'then I saw this'*, or *'then I saw that'* but he hadn't got a bible to check if he was right. He hadn't had a bible since he'd left Pamela. He'd go out and get one, then he could try to resolve the conundrum Max had left him.

****

It was as he drove home from the airport that Max's murder hit him. He would not be able to see or speak to him again. It seemed to him like a gaping hole had opened up in his life. He wondered why Max suddenly meant so much to him. After all, he'd only met him twice.

Yes, Max was charismatic. He had spirituality and an inner peace but that wasn't it. Max talked in a meaningful way about the contemplation of his faith. For Achille it was quite the opposite. He'd totally lapsed since his early twenties. Maybe there was a subconscious desire to refill that void?

Eight

During the following week Achille bought a copy of the Good News Bible. That evening at home, he checked his idea that Max's quotation about the king sitting on the throne might have come from the book of Revelation. He was surprisingly pleased to have guessed right. He found it in chapter four, verses two to six. Perhaps now he could attempt to resolve the rest of 'his' page in the folder that Max had left him. The third entry on 'his' page read 738: 4: 2 - 6, he had solved the 4: 2 - 6 but it started with the number 738? How could that mean the book of Revelation?

He was no Alan Juring but then the page was not produced on the *Enigma* machine either. Max had said it was simple. He thought for quite a while, then turned his attention to the first line - 77: 81: 8, to try and break the logjam in his mind. The 77 also seemed odd but he now knew that the 81 was probably the chapter and 8 the verse but which book had 81 chapters?

Consulting the list of contents, the two longest books in the bible were the book of Psalms and Isaiah. Turning to the appropriate pages, there were 150 Psalms and Isaiah had only 66 chapters, so it had to come from the 81st psalm? Turning to verse eight of the eighty-first Psalm, it took his mind back to what Max had actually said at the time, *Listen, my people, to my warning; Israel, how I wish you would listen to me!* But why did he start with 77 this time?

Numbering the letters of the alphabet 1 - 26 did not solve the problem as 7 = G? For 7 to equal both P and S, the short form for psalm, seemed most improbable but somehow it had to be so? He had to think quite a bit more, it was obviously something else? P is the 16th and S the 19th letter of the alphabet, where and how could they be linked and 'equal' seven?

He sat and thought again for quite a while, when suddenly the idea of a telephone dial came to mind as a possibility. He looked at his telephone to confirm there were groups of three and four letters but also something he'd never noticed before, the first group ABC started on the number 2, not 1. The four letters P Q R and S are all on key number 7. He then realised he'd solved the problem.

The next line read 467, 9: 17 and 10: 10, so if he was right, the first three numbers could represent, G H or I, followed by M N or O and finally P Q R or S? Studying the abbreviations in the list of contents in his bible and by a process of elimination, it slowly clarified. It could only be Hosea, chapter 9, verse 17, etc; which he then turned to. The moment he read it, again he clearly remembered Max saying it, *'The God I serve will reject his people, because they have not listened to Him'*: And secondly, *I will attack this sinful people and punish them* etc. The next line, starting 738 was now simple.

Having solved the problem of 'his' page, he turned back to the first page. This one had letter and number references, similar to those on his own sheet but not in the same code. He guessed the cryptographer in Max wouldn't have made it that easy for him to resolve.

He was busy at work for the next week. He realised that if he knew what each of the other four people had talked about with Max, it might make the task of de-ciphering the other pages easier. Even if he did manage to de-cipher the biblical quotes, they wouldn't tell him the ideas that they had prompted. He felt it was as if Max was pointing him towards understanding what he'd discussed - 'the secrets of life' as he'd called them in his letter? It seemed a logical step to try and meet the other people during his travels.

It was also probable that sub-consciously he felt short-changed with Max's untimely murder and wanted to hear what else Max had to say.

Apart from his own, there were only four other pages, so it didn't strike him as too big an undertaking. Fortunately three of the four were in Europe, within fairly easy reach of where he normally travelled, the fourth was in America and he could talk to him on the phone. He probably had to go to America in the next few months, on one of his occasional visits, so he might be able to fit in a visit to see him?

He decided to try and contact each of them, simply based on when his travels took him close to where they lived.

****

The first name and address on his list that coincided with where he happened to be going, was a Raffaella Alessio in Milan. Her sheet was the longest by far; it had twenty-two references, split into five groups.

He had to fly to Linate fairly regularly, as the nearest airport when he visited the factory in Lecco for product development meetings, most of which he now chaired.

On a couple of occasions he'd stayed in Milan overnight, when Alitalia had 24-hour lightning strikes. Once, after he found an hotel in Milan and booked-in, he took a taxi to La Scala to see what was on and if he could get a ticket. They were sold out but told him if he waited, he could get in at half price if there were any no-shows. He was lucky and listened to a magnificent Beethoven concert. It was this experience that gave him the idea of booking a box and taking Miriam on a later visit.

This time he stayed over on purpose and gambled on whether he could find Ms. Alessio? After the Friday meeting at the factory, he drove back to Milan as usual and once he was in his hotel he scanned the telephone directory he'd borrowed from reception. There were over forty Alessios!

His little bit of Italian was useless for such a task, so he asked at reception if they could help? After he explained his problem, saying he was prepared to pay for a helper's time as well as the calls, they asked one of the ladies on their switchboard who spoke quite good English if she would help?

The switchboard was not too busy and there were two operators, so it was agreed and he sat behind her as she worked her way through the list of numbers. He'd told her who he was looking for - a Raffaella Alessio who'd visited Solothurn some time in the past and hopefully spoke some English. About fifty-five minutes later, on the twenty-third call, they struck lucky; Ms. Alessio spoke very passable English. The operator transferred the call to a 'phone box in the hotel lobby for him.

He introduced himself, then asked if she'd met the hermit in the Verena gorge whilst she was there? Hearing her confirmation, he told her that the hermit had died and he was following up on some notes he'd left.

He explained he'd had a business meeting that day and stayed over on the off-chance of finding her and hoping that they might meet. She said she worked in her bookshop and Saturday was always her busiest day. Hearing the disappointment in his voice, she relented a little, saying that if he cared to come to the shop at eight thirty, she'd be happy to give him some time, as custom didn't usually start to pick up until around nine-thirty or ten. He readily agreed and took down the address.

The following morning he showed the taxi driver the piece of paper with the bookshop address and he took him there, arriving a little after eight thirty. When he entered the shop, Ms. Alessio and one of her assistants were already there. He apologised for being a little late, not having realised the distance involved, or what the traffic was like in Milan at that time of the morning.

Ms. Alessio briefly introduced him to her assistant, then took him to her office at the back of the shop. He guessed she was in her early fifties, dark haired, quite pretty, pleasant and very well dressed, - a typical businesswoman in fact. She offered him coffee.

"So tell me more about the hermit. He was quite a dear, I was so sorry to hear he'd died?"

"Well he was murdered actually, about six weeks ago and no one knows who did it or why, not even the police as yet. I recently learnt he was originally a cryptographer in the Swiss Diplomatic Service before he became a hermit. The notes he left contain your name, among others but he'd written his notes in some sort of code. I decided to contact as many of you as I can, hoping what you tell me will help me decipher them. I also hope that one or more of you might be able to throw some light on the mystery of his death. You're the first I've contacted".

"How very strange it all sounds, I fear you might have had a wasted journey Mr. Aarden. There was nothing at all mysterious about our conversation. It was four years ago last May that I went to see what the Solothurn Literature Festival had to offer. One of the presentations at the festival did not really interest me so, as it was a nice day, I decided to go for a walk. I'd seen some leaflets in the hotel; one or two were about the Verena gorge in the woods to the north of the town, I thought it would be nice to go there?

You obviously know it; it was very pretty in the late Spring. I thought about my meeting with the hermit after you called. He was working in his little garden when I got to that part of the gorge and I wished him a good afternoon. You can imagine my surprise when he replied in almost perfect Italian. He came over to the fence and we chatted a little about how he'd learnt Italian and why I was visiting Solothurn. He explained that he was not a monk, he just wanted a quiet contemplative life after his wife had died and he chose early retirement.

My being Italian naturally raised the subject of religion. He guessed I was probably a Catholic. I said I was but had lapsed. I told him it was impossible for me to believe that God created the universe in just six days with all the evidence that has emerged about evolution. I also said I couldn't believe that Adam and Eve were the first people on Earth. The bible says Adam had to cultivate the soil; his son Abel was a shepherd and his other son Cain was a farmer. Yet the first evidence found of cultivation, husbandry and farming in the Middle East, has been dated at around 9000 BC?"

My faith diminished, as I became aware of these matters, realising that one of these conflicting statements could not be true. We now know for a fact, that our ancestors first appeared on Earth over two million years ago.

"I agree with you", the hermit said, "it does seem impossible. Let me go and get us a drink then we can sit here and enjoy the sunshine while I tell you how I came to reconcile these same anomalies in my own mind. I can only offer you coffee or barley water. Which would you prefer?"

"Barley water would be nice, thanks". He returned with two glasses and I can still remember the gist of his lengthy reply. It went something like this:

'Take the Adam and Eve question first. I agree they were not the first people on Earth for the same reason as you. The bible says that Tubal Cain, I'm sure that was his name, one of their early descendants, made bronze and iron tools, yet the earliest evidence of this, in the Middle East, is dated about 4000 BC.

'As I thought about this problem and what the bible has to say, I finally came to a conclusion. I realised that God divided people into two distinct groups when he inspired the scribe of Genesis - humankind and mankind.

'Humankind came first, as you said, over two million years ago but they were corporeal and they were like advanced animals and had no soul. Mankind followed much, much later - in 3921 BC to be exact. I remember that figure because it is so precise and came as something of a surprise."

I asked him how he arrived at that figure and he said the

bible details all the generations from Adam to Abraham in Genesis and then from Abraham to the birth of Christ in St. Mathew's gospel.

Then he went on to tell me that he reached this conclusion about humankind and later mankind, on the evidence in the bible. The first clue was the fact that during the first five days of creation it says 'God commanded this or that, to happen'. But during the sixth day God said, "Now we will make human beings", thus implying a longer drawn out process, which we now call evolution. Later in the bible it says "He breathed life-giving breath and man began to live". I believe this is when he gave human beings a soul, thus creating Adam, the first man. Further support for this idea comes from the prophet Ezekiel, two of the psalms and the letter to the Hebrews. Then later, in Genesis, God actually named us mankind.

Then he went on to say "I also agree that creation could not have occurred in six days and we all know about evolution. The idea one needs to think about is how the book of Genesis came to be written.

Whoever wrote it was obviously not around when the world began, so he must have been inspired to write it. One of the extraordinary things about Genesis is the detail and the fact that it relates exactly the same sequence of events as we now understand them to have occurred from scientific study.

The scribe had no knowledge of today's science, yet he has been proved correct in all the essential details.

Now imagine you are inspired to write about something of which you have no knowledge. You would write it in words that you understood - words that you think reflect the image of the events being conveyed to you. The crux of the matter, I believe, is the scribe's choice of the word 'day'. If he'd said 'period', we'd have had no problem. I asked myself why should one rotation of the earth, twenty-four hours, be the criteria? Jupiter's 'day' is only about ten hours but moving to the other extreme, one rotation of our galaxy takes 225 million years.

Both offer a single rotation as a criteria, take your pick? The inspired scribe of Genesis simply knew of no other time span!"

Ms. Alessio finished telling her story by saying "it was quite strange Mr. Aarden. As I walked back into Solothurn, a feeling came over me; it was just like the story in St. Luke's gospel, the walk to Emmaus. You perhaps recall what two of Christ's disciples said, *"Wasn't it like a fire burning in us when he talked to us on the road and explained the Scriptures to us?"* That's exactly how I felt at that moment and I've returned to being a practicing Catholic ever since.

****

A few days after he got home, he was in a position to sit down and attempt to decipher the Raffaella Alessio document; his transcript ran to three pages.

The most common theme from her memory of what was said was the book of Genesis? All but five of the items listed on Max's sheet, started with 'Tra'? After playing around with it for quite a while, he realised that the letters G E N were displaced thirteen places from what one would expect. What he'd done was to write the first thirteen letters of the alphabet, A - M and then below them write the second thirteen, N - Z, Tra on one line corresponds to Gen on the other.

Having solved this version of Max's code, he could now write out his 'translation' with some certainty, as he'd done with his own sheet. He began to see how well they fitted with what Raffaella had told him. The first block of three references reflected the point that Adam and his early descendants must have come much later in humankind's evolution, certainly not at the very beginning.

Gen. 3: 23. *So the Lord God sent him out of the Garden of Eden and made him cultivate the soil.*

Gen. 4: 2. *Later she* (Eve) *gave birth to another son, Abel.*

Abel became a shepherd but Cain was a farmer.
Gen. 4: 20 - 22. *Adah gave birth to Jabal who was the ancestor of those who raise livestock and live in tents. His brother was Jubal, the ancestor of all musicians who played the harp and the flute. Zilla gave birth to Tubal Cain, who made all kinds of tools out of bronze and iron.*

The second group of four this time illustrated how Max had arrived at the figure of 3,921 years - the time gap between the creation of Adam and the birth of Christ.

Gen. 5: 3 - 32. *Adam was130 years old, he had a son who was like him and he named him Seth... When Seth was 105, he had a son, Enosh...etc. etc.* Then finally, *After Noah was 500 years old, he had three sons, Shem, Ham and Japeth.* (Achille added up the years, they totalled 1,556).
Gen. 11: 10 - 26. *These are the descendants of Shem. Two years after the flood, when Shem was 100 years old, he had a son, Arpachshad...etc.* Until he reached... *After Terah was 70 years old, he became the father of Abram.* (Another 390 years, raising the total to 1,946 years).
Gen. 12: 4. *When Abram was seventy-five years old... "This is the country I am going to give to your descendants...* (So Achille added another 75 years, making the new total 2,021).
Mt. 1: 2 - 17. *From Abraham to King David, the following ancestors are listed: Abraham, Isaac, Jacob, etc. From King David to the time when the people of Israel were taken into exile in Babylon, the following ancestors are listed: David, Solomon, Rehoboam, etc. From the time of the exile in Babylon to the birth of Christ, the following ancestors are listed: Jehoiachin, Shealtiel, Zerubbabel, etc.*

So then there were fourteen generations from Abraham to David and fourteen from David to the exile in Babylon and fourteen from then to the birth of the Messiah.

There were no years? But then Achille recalled that in the chart of biblical history, at the back of the bible he'd bought, it stated that Abraham came to Palestine c.1900 BC. (Adding this number gave Achille the figure of 3,921 years).

Achille did a little more arithmetic. There were 42 generations listed in the 1900-year period, so each generation averaged just a little over 45 years; this seemed reasonable as they appeared to live longer in those early days. The present day dictionary gives a generation as 30 to 33 years, so it seemed quite logical.

There were a total of eight references in the third group; these were Max's grounds for the premise that making human beings was to be a time consuming evolutionary process.

Gen. 1: 3. *Then God commanded, "Let there be light" - and light appeared.*

Gen. 1: 6. *Then God commanded, "Let there be a dome to divide the water etc".*

Gen. 1: 9. *Then God commanded, "Let the water below the sky come together in one place, etc".*

Gen. 1: 11. *Then He commanded, "Let the earth produce all kinds of plants, etc".*

Gen. 1: 14. *Then God commanded, "Let lights appear in the sky to separate day from night, etc".*

Gen. 1: 20. *Then God commanded, "Let the water be filled with many kinds of living beings, etc".*

Gen. 1: 24. *Then God commanded. "Let the earth produce all kinds of animal life, etc".*

Gen. 1: 26. *Then God said, "And now we will make human beings; etc".*

The fourth set of references, six in all, presented Max's case that God gave humankind a soul, thus creating Adam.

Gen. 2: 7. ...He breathed life-giving breath into his nostrils and the man began to live.

Ps. 8: 5. Yet you made him inferior only to yourself; you crowned him with glory and honour.

Ps. 104: 30. But when you give them breath (or send out your spirit), they are created; you give new life to the earth.

Ez. 36: 27. I will put my spirit in you and I will see to it that you follow my laws and keep all the commands I have given you.

Hab. 2: 6 - 7. Instead, as it is said somewhere in the scriptures: "What is man, O God, that you should think of him; mere man, that you should care for him? You made him for a little while lower than the angels; (I think Max saw this step as - humankind - ie *a little lower than the angels) you crowned him with glory and honour, etc".* (This then was the subsequent creation of mankind, supported by the next quote).

Strangely there was no reference, only a quotation for the next item, just as there was one on his own sheet but he was fairly sure it must come from one of the prophets?

You spoke, they were made. You sent forth your spirit and it formed them. (It certainly implies two distinct steps).

Finally there was just a single line stating that it was God who named us Mankind.

Gen. 5: 2. He created them male and female, blessed them and named them "Mankind".

Raffaella Alessio, Milan, Italy, 18th May 1970.

Achille was intrigued at how these twenty-two quotes clearly formed the basis of Max's ideas; they set the context for what Raffaella had told him. He began to understand why she had returned to her faith, what it meant to have the bible explained, to understand and be able to adopt someone's view of the truth.

He put these sheets into the folder behind Max's original Raphaella sheet, as he'd done after de-ciphering his own.

****

Nine

Inspector Lutzi called Achille at work. He told him they'd identified Max from the background he'd given him; his real name was Ulrich Hoffman.

He said the investigation had become quite complex, too involved to go into over the phone; he would explain all when they met. The purpose of his call was to ask if Achille could possibly visit sooner rather than later? He wanted to question him further about his discussions with Max, in the hope it would throw further light on his enquiries. Achille told him he had to come to Zurich in two weeks time and would try to rearrange his diary to fit in a visit to him.

The exploratory discussions at the manufacturers in Friedrichshafen had led to the need for substantive talks. These were scheduled for a week the following Thursday. Achille was able to re-arrange his diary, to take the Friday off so that he could go and see the Inspector. It would also give him the opportunity to try and visit another of Max's contacts - a Pia Schmidt in Luzern. He'd been struggling with yet another de-ciphering problem on her page and hoped a visit would provide some clues.

The business discussions in Friedrichshafen went well. He again dropped-off his colleagues at Kloten, had a quick meal there and then drove on to Solothurn that same evening. He arrived at the Ambassador hotel around ten, booked in and went to bed.

He decided to leave the car in the hotel car park and walk to the police station, arriving there just after nine. Within a few minutes he was given a coffee and shown into Inspector Lutzi's office. What the Inspector had to tell Achille came as quite a shock but the Inspector said he was quite old enough to hear the truth - yet another evil legacy of war and greed.

First of all he thanked Achille again for telling him about Max's earlier life, saying it did prove to be the key to discovering Max's identity. He approached the Swiss Foreign Office in Berne by phone initially, saying he was making enquiries about a recent murder and was having difficulty identifying the victim. He'd learned some background details about the victim, which indicated he might have been in the Diplomatic Service some years ago?

"They were very slow in coming back to me", he said, "but they were able to identify who he was from what I'd told them. The reason for the delay was that his file was classified and it took a couple of days before they were authorised to give me his name. Their attitude and the classified file told me that both he and they had secrets, which makes Max's reticence and alias understandable and his revelation to you all the more extraordinary?

"As soon as they gave me his name - Ulrich Hoffman, it jogged a dim and distant memory, a case that occurred when I was new to the force - a very junior policeman. I looked it up on our new computer system to see if my memory was accurate. It was.

"Having got the file reference, I went to our old, unsolved crime records and found the case file. It concerned the brutal torture and murder of a Mrs. Maureen Hoffman at her home in Berne in 1962. She was fifty-five. Yes, you've guessed it, Max, or should I say, Ulrich Hoffman was her husband.

"He was never a suspect as he was away on diplomatic business in Madrid at the time. I was not here then but remembered the case because it created quite a stir within the force and in the press. Some aspects were very distressing; they made the case notorious.

"First was the fact that Ulrich Hoffman literally vanished immediately after his wife's funeral and we never saw him again until now. Did he ever talk about his wife?"

"Just once. I think he said he became a hermit after his

wife had died. The way he said it, I didn't pursue the subject.

"The second aspect, revealed in the file, was that she was originally a British national, named Maureen Alcock. She was a multi-lingual secretary working at the British Embassy in Berne when they met and later married.

"These two facts and the Foreign Office attitude, make it probable that there was some cloak and dagger background to the Hoffmans which didn't come out at the time. Additionally, as I said, she was brutally tortured, presumably to extract whatever she knew?

"She was stripped naked and nailed through her hands and feet, spread-eagled on the wooden floor. There was clear evidence that a cloth gag had been put in her mouth at times. She was raped at least twice but the worst part was the use of sewing needles. She had blood and needle marks on her genitalia, needle tracks under some of her finger and toenails and quite a number over her breasts. She was found with a needle through each of her nipples. She was finally murdered by a dagger inserted into her upper abdomen and then thrust up into her heart.

"One can speculate that the torture lasted some considerable time, either because she held out, or she knew nothing of what they asked. I'm inclined to the latter as no known consequences followed. I don't think we'll ever solve the case. The detective in charge at the time suspected that some foreign agency must have been involved.

"As no doubt you appreciate, this clearly points to a probable motive for Ulrich's murder. I didn't tell you before but Ulrich was also tortured. He literally had strips of skin peeled from his body before he was finally killed in exactly the same way as his wife, probably the same unknown assailant?

"It was seventeen years after the war ended that Mrs. Hoffman was killed. Ulrich's murder had been a further thirteen years. Some person or group has shown enormous patience, has devoted much time and trouble to quietly trace, then torture and kill both the Hoffmans. There has to be a very valuable secret. Has it now been extracted I wonder?

"I'm determined to catch whoever's responsible for this despicable brutality and double murder, preferably before they can enjoy the reward of their labours. So tell me all you can about what Max told you?"

"Well where do I start? I only met him twice; the first time was in 1973. I'd come to Solothurn to visit the town and the *Eremitage;* a sentimental journey really. My mother brought me here in 1938 when I was rising five.

I met Max, sorry, Ulrich and we got talking and there seemed an instant rapport between us. I'd been comparing a photo my mother had given me, she took it on that visit, to see what, if any changes, had taken place in the last thirty-six years. He invited me in for a coffee.

Looking back on it, he seemed particularly interested in my family background; my mother was born here in Solothurn you see".

"Was she indeed?"

"Yes but after that had sunk in, we discussed to what extent the bible reflects the truth; he had some interesting things to say on that topic. After which I left, promising to come again but it was nine months before I was able to return.

Two things in particular surprised me. The fact that between my first and second visit, he and Canon Zimmerman had traced the baptismal dates of my mother and her two sisters. They also discovered that one of my aunts was Reverend Mother of a Benedictine convent in Davos, nursing TB patients. And they took the trouble to trace the names and date of my grandparent's wedding here in St. Urs in 1904."

"From what you've said, I can begin to see why he came to trust you with some of his secrets. He was perhaps ensuring that not only were you English but also that you could have no possible connection to his past. Probably he was fearful of being found by whoever killed his wife but, by the same token, he needed someone to trust; I wonder why?"

"I don't know about that but the second point I wanted to make is something he said that I thought a little strange at the time, let me explain. He'd studied politics in Berne, had a gift for languages and started in the Diplomatic Service as a translator. He then went into surprising detail about the political events in Germany that led to the Second World War. His memory for detail was astounding. He said these events upset him because he hated bullying and he found Swiss neutrality frustrating. He said he wanted to play a more active role, so changed jobs. But then he said he became a cipher clerk. I didn't see that as a more active role, one in which he could work off his frustration, so presumably that was just a cover? I didn't feel I could question him regarding this anomaly, I didn't know him well enough then".

"What you've told me adds to my gut feeling that the Hoffman murders are probably war related - it begins to indicate that an active cell of some sort, perhaps of Nazi origin, has been at work. One mustn't lose sight of the fact however that, apart from his service in England and Germany and hers in Switzerland until they married, his job took them to France, Italy and Spain in the post-war period as well. Is there anything else you can add?"

"I don't think so but I agree this all points to their involvement in some clandestine activity, privately motivated or otherwise. If that is the case, I can understand that your Foreign Office, being that of a neutral country, would not want to be open to questions".

"Thank you for coming Mr. Aarden, I really do appreciate your taking the trouble to come and see me again. I'll be in touch if I learn anything meaningful, particularly if I catch the murderers.

"I'm sure you will, catch the killers I mean; I wish you luck".

****

81

Achille finished with Inspector Lutzi before lunch, as he'd hoped. It took him a little over an hour to reach Luzern; it's about forty-five miles along parts of the N1 and N2 motorways. It's a lovely town at the western end of the Vierwaldstatter Sea, a lake sitting between the mountains like a reversed L; it's about twenty miles long.

He had wanted to get there early enough to look at the electoral register. He didn't want a repeat of a long telephone list - he'd assumed that Schmidts are as common as Smiths in England. In the event only three Schmidt families were listed but all were out when he tried to contact them. By then it was about four-thirty, so he presumed they were at work and decided to find a hotel for the night then call at their houses later that evening as the town is quite small.

After he'd found a hotel and booked in, he called Miriam for a chat and to tell her he loved her, then had an early evening meal. Pia's was the second home he visited. She lived in Felsbergstrasse, in a nice old house, a little north of the cathedral, near a small park. Her husband came to the door - Achille explained who he was and why he'd come. They were kind enough to invite him in.

After the initial pleasantries, Achille explained that Max was murdered and as a friend he was trying to piece together any information about his life that might be relevant. He asked Mrs. Schmidt if she'd be kind enough to tell him about her meeting with Max.

She explained that she worked for a company in the office supply business who'd held a sales and marketing conference in Solothurn the previous year. There was a free period on the Saturday afternoon; like a lot of Swiss people she'd heard of the hermits that had lived in the Verena gorge in the woods to the north of the town. It was said to be pretty, so she decided to walk there, rather than window-shop, and see if a hermit still lived there.

Max was tending the flowers in his window boxes when

she said hello, so he stopped what he was doing to talk to her. She assumed he was a religious man of some denomination and raised the question about which she and her husband's felt strongly - the declining ethos of the Western World.

"I said that it seems that greed rules, it's everyone for themselves, no thought for the other person. God is ignored perhaps, rather than rejected but this attitude is allowing evil to thrive. Selfishness dominates, whilst what little hope does remain is decaying towards despair with the help of drugs.

"Some seek security in possessions; others confuse happiness with pleasure. Yet others seek oblivion in alcohol or ever more frequently in drugs. Most young people bolster their ego with aggressive behaviour. There's no self-discipline, no sense of purpose, no work ethic, no respect for others and certainly no manners. I'm sorry, I do rather get on my hobbyhorse as Max found out. I asked him if he had any kind of answer to these declining standards.

"He surprised me by saying: It's something I've thought about quite a lot myself, I've come to think of the Western World as one of Satan's success stories. He went on to say, Mr. Aarden, that the West, as distinct from Africa or the East, has become too rich. Its need of the basic necessities of life has long since passed, so people now think - who needs God? He said Moses warned the Israelites about this long ago and went on to quote a particular biblical passage which I can't recall. It was something about not letting anyone get too rich. He also said that one of the Proverbs gives us a prayer, which is pertinent to the same point. Again, I can't remember the actual passage but it was about striking a balance, neither too rich or too poor, I think.

"By forgetting about, or ignoring God, the creator of mankind, people lay themselves open to temptation. Jesus was very clear on this point when talking to Simon and I do remember this from when I was telling Peter and we looked it up: "*Simon, Simon! Listen! Satan has received permission to test all of you, to separate the good from the bad, as a farmer separates the wheat from the chaff.*

"He went on to say 'I don't know how much of the bible you've read but it gives a very good example about being grateful for what we have. It's a story about Job. He was the richest man in the East. He had seven sons, three daughters and literally thousands of sheep, camels, cattle and donkeys. God gave Satan permission to test Job's dedication to the Lord but not to harm him. As a result, Job lost his seven sons and three daughters, all his sheep, camels, cattle and donkeys, then a storm swept in from the desert and wrecked his house as well, killing all his servants, bar one. He survived this first test, saying - *the Lord gave and now he's taken away. May his name be praised,* or something like that?

"Satan then asked permission to test his person; God agreed but would not allow Satan to kill him. Job's answer to Satan, after he'd suffered terribly, was that when God gives us something good we welcome it - so how can we complain when trouble comes?

"So you see Mr. Aarden, we have to be like Job, we can't complain to God about other people's choices. They make their choice - we make ours. We have to accept the challenge this presents, pray for them and do our best to help them by showing good example."

Mrs. Schmidt went on to say, "I came home, much more settled in my mind and particularly after discussing what Max had to say with my husband Peter. We looked-up the various passages in our bible, as I said. We don't have any children. We don't like what we see but we accept the way it is as a challenge, so we made our choice of what we should do.

I don't mean to brag but it changed us. Instead of complaining, we decided to take an active part in helping drug addicts to kick the habit as our contribution to the betterment of society. We work among the addicts on alternate weekends with another couple and one evening a week, here in Luzern.

****

After Achille got home he felt he could tackle the conundrum of Ulrich's page on Pia Schmidt. Ulrich had talked about Job, therefore the book of Job in the Old Testament was the obvious place to start.

Ulrich's reference was 18: 1: 1 - 2: 10, which he hadn't understood initially but now found it quite easily. It was chapter 1, verse1, to chapter 2,verse 10 in that book; but how did Job = 18?

Ulrich's earlier coding had led Achille astray; he'd become blinkered in stead of open-minded. He struggled with all the alternatives that he could think of, then finally, almost in despair of ever getting a solution, he found the answer; Job is the 18th book of the Old Testament. After that it was virtually plain sailing.

The first of Ulrich's quotations, read - 5, 8, 12 -14 which was Deuteronomy, the fifth book of the Old Testament, chapter 8, verses 12 - 14:

- *When you have all you want to eat and have built good houses to live in and when your cattle and sheep, your silver and gold and all your other possessions have increased, make sure that you do not become proud and forget the Lord.*

The second was from the book of Proverbs, the 20th book, chapter 30, verses 7 to 9:

- *I ask you, God, to let me have two things before I die: keep me from lying and let me be neither rich nor poor. So give me only as much food as I need. If I have more, I might say that I do not need you. But if I am poor, I might steal and bring disgrace on my God.*

And finally the 3rd book of the New Testament - N3, 22, 31 was St. Luke's gospel, chapter 22, verse 31, which Pia had remembered:

- *"Simon, Simon! Listen! Satan has received permission to test all of you, to separate the good from the bad, as a farmer separates the wheat from the chaff.*

Achille didn't write out the passage from the book of Job but paraphrased it because it was too long, almost two pages of the bible, even with its small print. It starts:

- *There was a man named Job, living in the land of Uz, who worshipped God and was faithful to him...*

It ends:

- *How can we complain when he sends us trouble?" In spite of everything he suffered, Job said nothing against God.*

Pia Schmidt, Luzern, Switzerland, 8th September 1973

****

Achille reflected on the fact that this was the second time he'd heard what a positive influence Ulrich had had on those who contacted him but Achille hadn't changed. He'd made his choice long ago, for better or worse.

Ten

In 1978 the 32nd annual meeting of the Post War Finance Committee was in progress. Two of its six members had replaced their predecessors but the Chairman and Secretary, now in their early seventies and late sixties, respectively, had served since its inception.

The highly secretive meeting was being held at the Hilton in Managua. The members had flown into Nicaragua over the previous three days.

The agenda this year, was a shorter list of topics than formerly, all were concerned with investment and finance.

There still remained the item concerning the untouched secret bank deposit box containing details of the accounts; namely the document stolen by Bruno Affleck in December '44. The secretary, Wolfgang Mack, who was sitting to the right of the Chairman, provided an update - the latest situation.

"A year ago I was able to report, that having spent too long looking in the diplomatic quarters of Rome, Paris, London and Madrid for traces of Ulrich Hoffman, we widened our search to other major cities. After fifteen years of persistent but discreet enquiries, we finally picked up an uncertain lead on Ulrich Hoffman in Spain.

You may recall that after his wife's funeral in 1962 he disappeared. Someone has been found who says he thinks he caught sight of him in Barcelona in the early 60s. We now know that when he was seen, it was during the first few weeks of his disappearance. We've discovered that he was purposely putting on weight, growing a moustache and beard, changing his hairstyle and altering the way he both carried himself and walked.

He then enrolled, as a lay brother, in the Benedictine monastery of Santa Maria de Montserrat; it's about forty kilometres north west of Barcelona. Whilst there he acquired the demeanour of a monk and of course wore the habit. After a year he left and disappeared once more.

One of the assumptions our people worked on was that he could well have chosen to return to Switzerland, so started making discreet enquiries around his home city of Berne. They finally learned that a hermit had gone to live in an empty hermitage, located in the Verena gorge just outside Solothurn, sometime in late 1963. It's about twenty-two kilometres north of Berne.

The timing, his new way of life and his appearance seemed to fit with our Spanish intelligence but there are no signs of affluence, quite the contrary. They became convinced however that this had to be our man, although he was known locally as Max Seiber.

The hermitage is close to a public footpath through the woods, so our people were severely limited as to the timing and duration of their visit. They went in at midnight, whilst he was asleep, aiming to leave by five, before there was a chance of an early walker. Due to the limited time available they woke, stripped and started on information extraction almost before he was fully awake.

In the process he confirmed his name really was Ulrich Hoffman. That he did some intelligence work on our VI's, VII's and our first jet fighter on behalf of the British, communicating in a secret code with his future wife; this tallies with what she told us. He confirmed that a man, whose name he didn't know but knew by sight as a member of the church congregation, had surreptitiously pushed a sheet of paper into his pocket one Sunday in early December '44. He claimed not to know what it was and waited to be contacted regarding it. About ten days later he heard that the man had been killed, became very frightened, did not want to jeopardise his imminent return home from Germany, so burnt it.

By this time he was bleeding quite profusely but in spite of their frantic efforts, they could not shake his story about burning the paper, nor could they get him to admit to making a copy. In a final effort to release further information, they slowly pushed a knife into his upper abdomen and even more slowly up into his heart; this was just before they left at 5.00 am.

The contents of the account details hidden in the security box are now estimated to be worth $88 million dollars. We've spent considerable time and money on finding it, not to say taken quite big risks and its value continues to rise.

Mecklenbeck interrupted by saying "Hoffman has lived in the Solothurn woods for the last thirteen years, surely he would have made one or more friends during that time. With a little extra time and effort, I think it would be worth discovering who they are and if he ever told them anything about this matter or even gave them anything."

After a short debate, it was agreed that they would persevere for another year.

****

Eleven

Achille thought it was about time he 'phoned Mr. Osrow, to see if it was possible to meet up in the next few months, depending on either of their travel schedules.

He assumed Mr. Osrow was an astronomer as the address was the Mount Palomar Observatory, California. His sheet was the shortest with only two entries, the first was written out in full, just as the others had been, on each of their three sheets, it read:

Do you know? Were you not told long ago? Have you not heard how the world began?' The second was given in yet another variation of Ulrich's codes?

He booked a person to person call through the international operator and finally spoke to him. To save confusing things for the moment, he used Ulrich's alias when he explained who he was and why he'd called. Mr. Osrow confirmed he'd met Max when he was on holiday in Europe seven years ago. He liked jazz and had gone to the Solothurn Jazz Festival held in August.

Achille told him Max had been murdered and he was following-up on a list of people he'd left in a folder. He was hoping to throw some light on the baffling mystery of his death, as well as understanding more about what he'd had to say. Could he tell him what they'd talked about?

"I don't think that what I can tell you will help your enquiries Mr. Aarden. We had a wonderful afternoon and evening. We really got along. Once I told him where I worked, he asked me lots of questions about astronomy. It was a subject he said he knew little about. He'd wanted to clarify his thinking on a variety of biblical topics. He explained that what he really wanted to do most of all was to use my knowledge of astronomical theories to try and put flesh on the bones of verses 1 - 5 in chapter one of Genesis. This led us into flights of fancy about how the initial process of creation could have taken place, what might have occurred and how?"

"I told him about some ideas that have impacted on astronomy in recent times. Hubble's red shift, Black Holes, Hawkins's 'Big Bang' theory and Einstein's theory of Relativity. We had a wonderful time - his ideas were uninhibited and very stimulating. It became a rather unusual brainstorming session really; my knowledge countered or even enhanced by his rather unusual suggestions."

"It sounds intriguing Mr. Osrow, I'd really like to meet if possible but I only visit my parent company on the west coast near Baltimore from time to time. Are you likely to come to Europe again?"

"When's your next visit to the USA scheduled?"

"I'm not sure yet, probably in a month or two's time, Why?

"Well, I'm due to go to an International conference in Washington ten weeks from now, if you can make it then we can arrange to meet."

"That sounds wonderful, much better than I expected. Give me the dates... Yes I've got that thanks, leave it with me and I'll get back to you if I can firm up on my visit to coincide with yours."

****

Achille's parent company headquarters were to the north of Baltimore, so it was only a 90 minute drive round the Baltimore beltway and down Interstate 95 to Washington. He'd done it before when arriving or leaving via Dulles airport.

They met for dinner on the Friday evening in Mr. Osrow's hotel; Achille having insisted it was to be his treat. They soon got on to Christian name terms over drinks and then at dinner Leonard told him about his brainstorming session with Ulrich. Leonard said he explained some of the emergent ideas that have impacted on astronomy in more recent times.

91

There was Hubble's progressive red shift in light from ever more distant stars, showing an expanding universe. Black Holes in space where gravity is so great that not even light can escape, eventually collapsing into what they call a 'Singularity' from extraordinary gravitational forces. Then Professor Hawkins's 'Big Bang' theory which put this Black Hole concept into reverse - the universe starting as an exceedingly dense 'Singularity', that then exploded to distribute matter across space, to create the universe.

"I also talked of Einstein's theory of 'Relativity' and his conjecture that the speed of light is a constant that can never be exceeded. We had a wonderful afternoon and evening, with much conjecture on both sides - his ideas were most stimulating."

"Such as?"

"Well the first was 'off the wall' as we say. He stated that the bible tells him that Adam was created 3,921 years before the birth of Christ. He'd found, that if he doubled it twenty times, he arrived at a figure of almost eight and a quarter billion years BC for the 'Big Bang'. What he'd arrived at, fitted with the known timescale of the Earth and mankind's evolution, he said.

This led us to a second conjecture, that the 'Big Bang' must have produced radiation well above the current speed of light, if the size of the universe is to be believed. I don't think such a conjecture breaks Einstein's theory, in fact there are some that argue for VSL theory, that is the 'Variable Speed of Light'. Additionally this idea would tend to fit with an Einstein statement that he never pursued; namely "the speed of light is affected by gravity, so it could have slowed down as all the matter of the universe was formed. Black Holes prove that light is in fact slowed, even to a stop, by enormous gravitational forces. So, as you can see, we were into the realms of revolutionary thinking indeed."

They talked late into the night, Leonard explaining more of

the detail, which Achille's firm foundation in schoolboy physics just about enabled him to follow. Achille was intrigued by the fact that Ulrich could get so involved in such matters and thanked Leonard for his patient explanations.

Achille flew up to Boston on the Saturday morning to meet Miriam, so they could have their planned and well-earned holiday in New England.

****

Miriam had caught flight BA 213, at ten-forty, to Boston that same Saturday morning. She'd been looking forward to seeing something of America for the first time and sharing the experience with Achille.

She spent her time reading a little on the flight and listening to music, interrupted by lunch and afternoon tea. By design or coincidence, when she first caught sight of land, which she assumed was Newfoundland, Dvorak's ninth symphony had just started. As she listened, she heard it afresh, it 'spoke' to her of America. This impending visit added to her enjoyment of the New World symphony, which was to become a treasured memory.

About an hour or so later the engines were throttled back and they began their descent. She started to see built-up areas from a few thousand feet, then finally saw Boston laid out below, as they turned onto the final approach to land. There was a screech of rubber as the undercarriage touched the runway; she'd landed at Boston's Logan Airport at one-thirty local time. She queued at immigration, waited a while for her suitcase and then was filled with joy when she saw Achille waiting for her. They gave each other a hug and a kiss, then headed for the car park.

Miriam woke early next morning, not yet acclimatised to the new time; she understood it normally took two or three days. She rose quietly, so as not to disturb Achille. She noticed a couple of maps on the table. It seemed that Achille had been thinking about where they might go after she'd gone to bed early as a result of her twenty-nine-hour day.

She picked one up that covered Connecticut, Massachusetts and Rhode Island. Marvelled at the fact that each was divided from the other almost entirely by straight lines and very little by geographical features. When she looked around the Boston area she could see why it was called New England. There were so many recognisable place names - Cambridge, Braintree, Weymouth and Wakefield and, slightly further away, Gloucester, Newbury and Ipswich; further still were Plymouth, Falmouth and many others.

They had a wonderful holiday touring New England before flying back overnight on BA212, which left at 6.05 pm the following Saturday. Miriam had really enjoyed what she'd seen of America and hoped they could see more in the future.

****

Achille didn't have much of a problem deciphering the second entry on Leonard's sheet - it had to be Genesis, chapter one, verses one to five. What it actually read was 20, 22, 13, 1, 1 - 5.? Achille thought for a while, then realised 'G' was the seventh letter of the alphabet, not the twentieth. He finally reached the conclusion that Ulrich had numbered the alphabet backwards - Z as 1 and A as 26, 'G' became 20, 'E' was 22 and 'N' was 13.

Achille then wrote on his 'interpretation' sheet: -

This first entry makes it clear that Ulrich was addressing the very beginning of time. When I was looking in the bible for another quote, I happened to come across the one used by

Ulrich. It was from Isaiah, chapter 40, verse 28:

- Do you know? Were you not told long ago? Have you not heard how the world began?'

The second reference simply gives the context of Ulrich's discussion with Leonard Osrow:

- In the beginning, when God created the universe, the earth was formless and desolate. The raging ocean that covered everything was engulfed in total darkness, an awesome wind was moving over the water. Then God commanded, "Let there be light" - and light appeared. God was pleased with what he saw. Then he separated the light from the darkness and he named the light "Day" and the darkness "Night". Evening passed and morning came - that was the first day.
   Leonard Osrow, Mount Palomar Observatory, California, USA.

22nd August 1968

As Achille filed this new sheet behind Ulrich's original, he noticed that the date given for the discussion was the 22nd August 1968. But Leonard had clearly stated that he'd visited Max seven years before, that would made it 1970, or '71. How odd?

Twelve

The company Achille worked for had a factory in France, on the southern outskirts of Lyon, at a place called Dardilly. He went there once a quarter for product development meetings. It was a bit awkward originally because there were no direct flights to Lyon; the traffic density was not high enough. He either had to go via Paris and change to an Air Inter flight or fly to Geneva and drive. He drove from Geneva once or twice. It took time but he did see some of the beautiful countryside and the lovely old town of Annecy.

He used to stay in the city, at the Sofitel but the drive to Dardilly in the morning rush hour was a real bind. He changed to a Novotel in Dardilly - not five star, quite basic but much more convenient. He once had to spend a whole week there in bed with the flu. Time really dragged although a couple of his colleagues' wives were kind enough to come and visit him.

Some two months after his visit to America, Achille was scheduled to go to Lyon. By then it had a new airport called Satolas with direct flights by British Airways BAC 111's.

The final person on his list for a visit was a Professor Deveraux. Achille made enquiries about him by phone and found that he taught at Lyons university. When he finally spoke to him he agreed to see him on a Sunday afternoon / evening as Achille had a Monday meeting in Dardilly. Lyons is a beautiful old city with two rivers, the Saone and the Rhone, and some very fine restaurants. The University is on the bank of the Rhone but the Professor agreed to meet Achille at his private address.

He flew down much earlier than was usual on the Sunday and following the Lyon street map, found the Professor's home on the Rue Montgolfier. He made Achille very welcome. He was a history professor specialising in French history but he seemed to have wide-ranging interests.

He'd lost his wife a few years before Achille's visit. Just prior to the first anniversary of her death he decided he must get away to avoid moping around at home. One of his interests was opera. It was that which took him to Solothurn in the July.

Whilst there, he took an afternoon stroll in the woods and came upon the hermitage. He said good afternoon to Max who was working in the garden. As they chatted about the opera programme being performed in the open air, Max invited him to have a cup of tea.

He told Max he'd lost his wife and felt he needed to get away. Ulrich sympathised, saying he understood having lost his own wife some years ago.

The professor went on to tell Max that he'd studied and then taught history for most of his life but his loss made him think more about the future. Not only in personal terms but also about where current trends are leading mankind? He posed the question, semi-rhetorically, musing and wondering if life would continue on for thousands, if not millions of years to come or would it come to an end sooner. If so, how and when might it be?

He told Achille that Max chose to answer very fully indeed, largely based on his detailed knowledge of the bible. "In hindsight, what he had to say was quite awe-inspiring. I'll try to convey to you his insights, enthusiasm and vision. It's a while ago now but I think I can remember most of it, not the biblical quotations themselves of course but perhaps the gist of them.

"Max started by telling me, "I once devised a working hypothesis, based on the period of 3,921 years, between the creation of Adam and Eve and the birth of Christ as mainly recorded in Genesis. One can't be absolutely sure of this figure as it contains 1900 years that biblical scholars estimate as the amount of time between Abraham's arrival in Palestine and the birth of Christ.

"An American astronomer visited me a few years ago. He thought my hypothesis had some merit, in fact the astronomer got quite excited on one or two points. During an afternoon and evening together we enlarged on the first part of the book of Genesis, adding the theory about the Big bang and other ideas of which I had only been vaguely aware.

"At the time I worked out my steps of time idea, which we renamed 'The Half-Life of Time.' I concluded that there would be a total of thirty-three steps altogether - each half the length of the previous step. We're currently in step twenty-three. It fits well with the biblical record, he said, from the creation of the Universe over eight billion years ago, to the end of this world some time early in the fortieth century. One doesn't mean to be too precise as the prophet Micah said that God frowned on forecasts."

Then the professor stopped talking about what Max had said saying, 'I'll just stop for a moment Mr. Aarden, I've been wondering about his 'Half-life-of-time idea. It fascinates me, I found what he had to say very stimulating. I'd like to delve into his ideas a bit more; it would be a real change from my kind of history. I think I'd like to try and work it out for myself. Have you been in touch with the astronomer he spoke of by any chance?"

"As a matter of fact I have," Achille said, "I met him in America only a couple of months ago, when I was there on business. I'll tell you the gist of what he said later if you like?"

"Wonderful, I'll look forward to it." Then he continued telling Achille about his time with Max.

"Max said, "We do know quite a bit about the future from the bible. I think that there are at least sixty references, maybe more, I haven't actually counted them. He then elaborated on his ideas about the future that had evolved from the variety of biblical texts. He said the earth would not last forever. It will wear out, something like that.

"Christ talked of signs that will indicate the coming of the end of the world. He told the parable of the fig tree as a precursor of summer - clouds that harbinger rain or a southerly wind that tells us it will become warm.

"I've told numerous visitors that God's not in a hurry, almost none of what he had to say about the future has happened yet; otherwise it would all have been over long ago. No, the end will be spread over very many generations. St. Peter tells us that a thousand years is like a day to God. The end may seem a slow process to us - but it will take place. God wants to give everyone the opportunity to turn away from evil and turn to him. The universe is at least eight billion years old, so to God even a thousand years is, at the very most, only one eight millionth of the time He created. Max went on to say that he believed that the signs to which the bible refers began to occur earlier this century, the beginning of the end.

"We've had two unprecedented World Wars this century. In the beginning God put us in charge of the fish but in 1958 England had the 'Cod War' with Iceland, as it was called. Twenty years later the problem is still with us and more widespread because we're greedy. The world continues to over-fish. These, I think, are the earliest warning signs - worldwide conflicts and a shortage of food. What a profound way to warn mankind?

"More recently, the phrase 'Limits to Growth' has been coined, a reflection of mankind's recognition that there is a finite limit to the earth's resources. Not only of fish but our supply of raw materials as well. We're consuming them at a prodigious rate with no thought for tomorrow - some of the proverbs tell us how foolish and lacking in wisdom we are. Will we ever learn?

"If one meditates on these things, even briefly, one recognises that there must be a finite amount of metal ore and chemicals as well as coal, gas and oil in the earth - so all will eventually be consumed. In the case of carbon fuels, that might not be a bad thing because, if mankind isn't forced to stop by running out, burning too much too quickly for too long, could permanently upset our climate.

"Just think about the future when India and China's economic growth is added to that of Europe, America, South Africa and Australia. Fossil fuel consumption could continue to grow exponentially for decades, pouring ever-more carbon dioxide into the atmosphere.

"It trapped sunlight in the Silurian and Devonian periods of our planet caused the temperature to rise substantially leading into the Carboniferous period - if carbon fuels didn't run out it could happen again and then where would we be? In fact I'm increasingly sure that this kind of climate problem is just around the corner, because of biblical references to it. Scorching winds and drought in some places, rain, floods and rising sea levels in others. These signs will be a further warning of the end to come. Scripture talks of real trials and tribulations for mankind from volcanoes or atomic weapons, possibly both - all will lead to devastation.

"Materialism and mindless consumption is fast becoming the norm, with little or no regard for the consequences. I foresee an apocalyptic climax towards the end of the twenty-first century. Coal, oil and gas supplies will have virtually run out, as well as a number of metals and minerals.

"As a consequence, mankind's standard of living will decline dramatically. Labour-saving devices and motor cars will become too expensive to own and operate and will slowly disappear. Mankind will be forced to return to the living conditions of the eighteenth century or even earlier. It will become the kind of life that was lived before the industrial revolution, with all the associated hardships of that time.

"Millions will die from natural disasters, to which one must add starvation due to loss of land from flooding and poor weather for crops. History tells us that those who survive will turn to God in their distress. It's been a natural reaction when one loses loved ones in times of great distress. Mankind will be taught a very harsh lesson for its foolishness."

"That's quite a startling and depressing picture painted by

Max or should I now say Ulrich? Thanks for telling me about it - it's interesting and a bit of a distressing scenario, if he's right. Perhaps I should tell you about my visit to Mr. Osrow, to cheer us up again?"

"Yes, that would be good. Look, you're not in a rush are you? Why don't you stay for an evening meal, I'll open a bottle of wine and then we can chat about that and anything else that comes to mind.

"Well, if you're sure it's not too much trouble, I'd like that, It's much more attractive than an evening in the Novotel."

On the way to the hotel later that evening, Achille thought how much he liked the Professor. They were kindred spirits and had soon got on to Christian name terms.

He thought again about what a frightening prospect Ulrich had outlined for those living through the twenty-first century and beyond. He was drawn like a moth to light by Ulrich's ideas on the future and the beginning of time was a new area of history that seemed to fascinate Pascal. It was probably the fact that history of any kind was in his blood?

The way things were shaping up, Ulrich did seem to be right about global warming and deteriorating weather patterns. The picture of progressive global disaster and its effect on people, chimed with Achille's spiritual distress when he pondered his own mortality. The pressure on his conscience was beginning to tell?

The more he thought about Ulrich's ideas, the more he wished he'd been able to see him a few more times. He was a unique person. He and the others he'd spoken to had remembered so much of what Ulrich had said. He must have meditated a great deal to interpret so many passages of the bible and to talk knowledgably and at length on so many different topics."

****

Pascal's sheet of references had fourteen entries. This time Achille found that Ulrich had transposed the biblical reference letters into numbers and vice versa, the numerical references into letters, using the phone dial code. That particular code offered three or four choices for each number, so it took Achille quite a long time to work them out, look them up and then type them onto an interpretation sheet.

There were five individual references, a pair of alternatives, as well as one group of three and another group of four. The sheet read: -

Forecasts are invariably wrong, the question always is, by how much?

Mic. 3: 7. - Those who predict the future will be disgraced by their failure. They will be humiliated because God does not answer them.

The world does not contain infinite resources:

Is. 51: 6. - The heavens will disappear like smoke; the earth will wear out like old clothing and all its people will die like flies.

We know the seasons and recognise weather patterns but we are reluctant to recognise the warning signs of our own vulnerability:

Mt. 24: 32 -33. - "Let the fig tree teach you a lesson. When its branches become green and tender and it starts putting out leaves, you know that summer is near. In the same way, when you see all these things, you will know that the time is near, ready to begin.

Or:

Lk. 12: 54 - 56. - When you see a cloud coming up in the west, at once you say that it is going to rain - and so it does. And when you feel the south wind blowing, you say that it is going to get hot - and it does. Hypocrites! You can look at the earth and the sky and predict the weather; why, then, don't you know the meaning of the present time?

Our lifespan is short: God's was, is and will be forever. What we perceive as a lifetime, is but an instant in His eyes:

2 Pet. 3: 8 - 9. - But do not forget one thing, my dear friends! There is no difference in the Lord's sight between one day and a thousand years; to him the two are the same. The Lord is not slow to do what he has promised as some think. Instead he is patient with you, because he does not want anyone to be destroyed but wants all to turn away from their sin.

The sense of history-in-the-making appealed to Pascal:

Hab. 2: 3. - Put it in writing, because it is not yet time for it to come true. But the time is coming quickly and what I show you will come true. It may seem slow in coming but wait for it; it will certainly take place and it will not be delayed.

Even renewable resources are vulnerable to greed:

Gen. 1: 28. - I am putting you in charge of the fish.

Individually we may have learnt to live within our means but collectively we signally fail: -

Prov. 1:7. - Stupid people have no respect for wisdom and refuse to learn.

Prov. 1:22. - Foolish people! How long do you want to be foolish? How long will you enjoy pouring scorn on knowledge? Will you never learn?

Prov. 8: 5. - Are you immature? Learn to be mature. Are you foolish?

Learn to have sense.

Climate change - the next great warning sign: -

Jer. 4: 11 - 12. - The time is coming... a scorching wind is blowing in from the desert towards them. It will not be a gentle wind that only blows away the chaff - the wind that comes at the Lord's command will be much stronger than that!

Amos. 4: 9.- "I sent a scorching wind to dry up your crops. The locusts ate up all your gardens and vineyards, your fig trees and olive trees."

Is. 24: 18 - 19. - Torrents of rain will pour from the sky and earth's foundations will shake. The earth will crack and shatter and split open.

Mt. 24: 7. - There will be famine and earthquakes everywhere.

Prof. Deveraux, Lyon, France. 12th July 1976

****

Thirteen

The 33rd annual meeting of the Post War Finance Committee of 1979 was in progress. In view of the time that had passed since the end of the war and the age of the members, they had decided to meet in Vienna, one last chance to secretly visit Europe. As always, it was organised with great care and attention to detail.

The old chairman, Heinz Gasser had died suddenly and the first order of business was the election of his replacement. Otto Altmann, almost ten years his junior, was elected. He in turn accepted the resignation of Wolfgang Mack, who was also old and still shocked by the sudden death of his friend. Electing his replacement was added to the agenda under any other business.

Some way through the agenda Otto Altmann said, "and now we come to the vexed question of the Hoffman deceit. Would you kindly tell us if we've made any further progress in this matter Wolfgang?"

"I'm glad to report that we have. Our investigators established that Canon Zimmerman, a priest at St. Ursen's Cathedral in Solothurn, was his closest friend. Almost without fail Hoffman went to have coffee with him every Friday and Sunday, for the last ten years at least, usually staying an hour or more each time for a chat.

The Canon had a housekeeper and received many visitors, mainly parishioners. He was very popular and rarely ventured out as he was quite old and frail. Our special projects team finally managed to bundle him into a car one evening without being seen. They took him out of town into a quiet area of countryside where they persuaded him to talk. He told them that Hoffman, alias Max Seiber, had left a thin, A4 sized packet for an Englishman named Achille Aarden. Unfortunately he had a heart attack at that point and died, so he was abandoned in a ditch at the side of the road.

So at last we have a positive lead in place of a maybe. We've now set out to trace this man and his A4 pack. I am hopeful that my successor will be able to report a final and successful resolution of this enduring problem.

****

Fourteen

Dear Achille,

It was nice talking on the phone; thanks for giving me Leonard Osrow's address and 'phone number, I spoke to him at some length. As a result I've now reproduced Ulrich's thirty-three steps of time.

Since we met I have been doing a lot of research into the formation of the world and the evolution of its flora and fauna. Armed with Ulrich's thirty-three steps of time and my new areas of evolutionary knowledge, I've started to write a lengthy version of the first chapter of Genesis (the actual biblical text from the Good News bible is in Italics). I've incorporated the ideas generated by Leonard and Ulrich in their discussion, particularly the challenging ideas on which Ulrich hypothesised.

So far I've completed Day One (enclosed) and look forward to any comments or observations you might have. I've also sent a copy to Leonard for the same reason.

My kindest regards.

Pascal

Day One

Do you know? Were you not told long ago? Have you not heard how the world began?

In the beginning, when God began to create the universe, eight billion, two hundred and twenty-two million, nine hundred and twenty-eight thousand, seven hundred and sixty-nine years ago, God created a Singularity.

Where there was nothing, suddenly a Singularity existed in the very first millisecond of time. The greatest event ever, the first instant of the first aeon that began the creation of time, space and the universe. It was an unimaginably dense kernel of energy that seemingly burst from nowhere into the void, spreading out at phenomenal speed. *The Earth did not exist;* the explosion creating space was, as yet, *formless and desolate.*

Possibly expanding at two, three, or even four times faster than the present speed of light, the electro-magnetic energy spread at a speed that God only knows? It streaked across the void like a hurricane. The space being created was like *the raging ocean* magnified millions of times, a gigantic tempestuous fury *that covered everything.* A maelstrom of energy that *was engulfed in total darkness and* it was like *an awesome wind* that *was moving over the water,* creating wave after wave of expanding space.

This stupendous burst of radiant energy was beyond comprehension, beyond any human imagining, beyond the idea of a billion tempestuous hurricanes. A phenomenal force, creating matter in its simplest form. (On re-reading it, I would add that Einstein predicted that as nothing can go faster than the speed of light, all added energy simply creates mass). Its speed slowly diminished over time, due to the emergence of gravity, generated by matter - the matter being hydrogen, the least complex of the atoms, the first on the atomic scale, the basic building block of the universe.

It took hundreds of thousands, probably hundreds of millions or perhaps even as much as a billion years, for countless trillions upon trillions of hydrogen molecules to fill the ever-expanding space. The great waves of energy created ripples, which caused the hydrogen to form into millions of 'clouds', some huge, some enormous, some immense! *Then God commanded "Let there be light,"* and gravity played it's part.

Gravity caused the clouds of hydrogen to begin to contract - extremely slowly at first. After perhaps a further two or three hundred million years, the more concentrated mass that was each cloud, produced an increase in the strength of the gravitational force within. Thus the slow process of galaxy formation began. The ever-increasing gravitational force that was generated by ever-greater density built growing pressure within the centre of each cloud. In turn this caused the temperature to rise. Ultimately the temperature and pressure within this core became great enough for spontaneous nuclear fission to begin, creating light - *and light appeared.*

The continuing nuclear reaction transmuted hydrogen into helium. Each cloud was like an awesome nuclear reactor, forming that second step on the elemental scale. As the magnitude of the nuclear reaction grew, feeding upon itself, it escalated until it was hot enough to make a second step, transmuting helium into lithium, then lithium into beryllium, beryllium to boron, boron to carbon and so on it went. This was the building process that was to create the ninety-two natural elements of the periodic table. *God was pleased with what he saw.*

Then He separated the light from the darkness by creating rotation. Just as skaters increase their speed of rotation by drawing in their arms, so the clouds of gas began to rotate a little faster as gravity increased their density and reduced their overall diameter. This rotation is the universal mechanism that produced periods of light and dark and *He named the light "Day" and the darkness "Night".*

The cores of the denser clouds continued to build in the intensity of their nuclear reaction, eventually becoming boiling cauldrons of atomic energy in space. The nuclear reactions now generating progressively heavier elements such as iron, cobalt, nickel, copper and zinc. These cores were being continuously fed by gravity, with ever more hydrogen from the immensity of the cloud surrounding each. This process continued inexorably as the increasing power of gravity attracted ever-greater quantities of hydrogen.

Eventually the clouds became so dense that they formed "Black Holes", clouds so dense, where gravity became so great, not even light could escape! The continuing nuclear process produced even heavier elements such as molybdenum, tin, silver, caesium, barium, samarium and gold. The timescale of each cloud's development varied as a function of the time to form the original cloud and its size. All were pregnant galaxies in the making, at some point in time, each with a differing gestation period.

As the Black Holes grew ever larger, they became white-hot cauldrons of energy where the temperature rose immeasurably to millions of degrees. The elemental formation process continued, finally creating the elements at the heaviest end of the periodic table, such as mercury, lead, radium, thorium and uranium. This phenomenal maelstrom of boiling matter is almost beyond human imagining; it progressed to producing cocktails of elements, hundreds and even thousands of combinations of chemicals and exotic compounds. With a virtually limitless supply of hydrogen in space, the building process still continued relentlessly.

Eventually and finally, the density became so great the

Black Holes progressed to form "Supermassive Black Holes", unimaginably large, dense and immense volumes of apparent darkness from without but none-the-less a boiling, seething mass of elements, at white heat within.

This unprecedented nuclear activity reached ginormous proportions, as the continuing supply of hydrogen in the original cloud was running low. Each Black Hole, a maelstrom of violent atomic activity, possibly reaching 20 million degrees centigrade when galaxy gestation was complete. The moment of 'birth' had arrived - each of the 'clouds' finally exploded into galaxies, first one, then another, until their number grew to millions over the aeons of time. Each was a truly massive explosion of such enormous proportions that each threw out great showers of suns, typically one to two hundred billion in a single galaxy! Our 'Milky Way' is just one of these galaxies, measuring about one hundred thousand light years in diameter!

The violence of this huge, enormously large explosion threw matter so far out that the residual Black Hole at its core could no longer "feed" on the matter surrounding it. The centripetal force of gravity was reduced by sheer distance and was now balanced by the centrifugal force of rotation.

From a gestation process that had lasted three point two billion years, our sun was created within the 'Milky Way' some five billion years ago. It was thrown out about 27,000 light years from the centre of our galaxy on to what is the inner edge of one of the arms of our spiral galaxy, which is called 'Carina-Centauri'. The nearest sun to ours is the star 'Proxima Centauri', about four and a half light years away.

In addition to all the suns that we call stars, there was a host of smaller matter. White-hot fragments, thrown out in the same explosion. Unlike the sun, these were not large enough to maintain nuclear fission. Some of this matter circled our sun and became the building material of Earth and all the other planets. The larger pieces were massive enough to attract smaller pieces by gravity so building the planets of our solar system, from Mercury to Neptune and the plutons, such as Ceres, Pluto and Katrina. Our Earth formed in this way some four point six billion years ago. It was the beginning of what we now call the Archezoic Period of the Precambrian Era.

All the planets were red-hot balls of bubbling matter in space. They slowly cooled, the rate dependant on how far they were from the sun and on how much radioactive material they contained. The faster cooling outer layer of our Earth, exposed to the frigidity of space, slowly formed a crust. The crust finally became deep enough and strong enough to withstand the impact of smaller meteorites which were attracted to it. This prevented rocks from penetrating to the molten core of the Earth. The oldest of these rocks found, has been carbon dated at 4.55 billion years old. The Earth's crust finally became cool enough, deep enough, rigid enough and strong enough for the next stage of God's plan. It was the end of step one and the beginning of step two of time.

Half of time had passed - in total, four billion, one hundred and eleven million, four hundred and sixty-two thousand, five hundred and twenty-nine years. Exactly the same amount of time remained.

Evening passed and morning came - that was the first day.

****

Fifteen

It was two or three months after seeing Pascal Deveraux, that Achille got a call at work. It was from Inspector Lutzi.

"Sorry to contact you at work Mr. Aarden," he said, "I phoned your home first and your wife told me you were at the office, I hope you don't mind? I've got some disturbing news, Canon Zimmerman was found dead yesterday."

"I'm so sorry to hear that, I only met him a couple of times. He was a nice man. I guess he was quite old but he certainly didn't look to be at death's door - what did he die of?"

"That's the point of my call. We're pretty sure it was manslaughter if not murder. Someone walking their dog found him in a drainage ditch at the side of the road about two kilometres outside Solothurn. The autopsy showed he died of a heart attack. Apparently he'd suffered from a weak heart for some years. What makes us think it was manslaughter is the fact that we found needle marks under four of his nails on his right hand. We think he was being tortured when he had a heart attack. The needle marks also make us think it is linked to the deaths of Mr. and Mrs. Hoffman."

"Gosh, how terrible but why are you calling to tell me? It doesn't sound as if this is just a courtesy call."

"You're quite right Mr. Aarden it's not. You are aware that our Foreign Office is not being cooperative. We decided therefore, to advertise nationally for anyone who'd met Max Seiber, who'd had more than a brief conversation with him in the last ten to fifteen years. We only got five replies; all were interviewed but nothing more of his background emerged, so we've reached a dead end again, so to speak.

We reluctantly decided there was nothing more we could do, so we'd closed the investigation with the tentative conclusion that the two Hoffman murders were probably due to an untraced ex-Nazi group taking revenge for whatever espionage work they'd done during the war.

This new murder puts a different complexion on things. We now think they were tortured and murdered for information, not just revenge. Canon Zimmerman was Ulrich Hoffman's closest friend. They must have thought that Hoffman could have passed-on whatever secret they're after. We know you were a unique contact because you are the only one we've met to whom he told some of his background.

I've phoned you for two reasons. First, to ask if Hoffman gave you anything? And second to warn you that you could be in danger if Canon Zimmerman gave them your name and they traced you."

"Yes he did give me something, not directly but bequeathed it to me via Canon Zimmerman, to be given to me in the event of his death. The Canon gave it to me when I went too see him after Ulrich's murder."

"I'm glad you told me that. We suspected you had something because one of the people who came forward was a Mrs. Schmidt of Luzern. She said you'd been to see her. You wouldn't have known her otherwise. Why didn't you tell me about it before?"

"Well it didn't seem at all relevant. It was simply a loose-leaf folder containing a brief letter and five sets of biblical quotations. One had my name on it and the quotes were relevant to our discussions. So I decided to contact the other four during my business travels to see what they'd discussed with him. I've contacted all four of them now and none seem to have any bearing on his or the other murders."

"I'm disappointed in you Mr. Aarden. You seem honest enough but surely it's not your place to judge what is or is not relevant to the case."

"I'm sorry you feel that way Inspector, they were left to me and seem to have no bearing on the case. I'll happily send you copies so you can see for yourself. They're all to do with differing aspects of life on earth and its purpose, within a biblical and religious context.

Obviously I know about Mrs. Schmidt Inspector but tell me, were the other four who answered your advertisement all on a similar theme?"

"As a matter of fact they were."

"Well that confirms what I thought, doesn't it? Is it possible that you could send me copies of what was said at the interviews, I've found Ulrich's thoughts about the bible, religion and life, quite fascinating?"

"I'll have to think about that. You withheld information from me, vital or not, you should have told me about the folder you know."

"Yes, I'm sorry, I'll send you copies, I'll run them off on my computer this evening."

The call sent Achille's mind into a whirl, flooded with a jumble of competing thoughts. The call forced Achille to finally face the fact that Ulrich had probably passed his secret on to him but he'd de-coded all the sheets?

Originally it had been a vague possibility but as his own investigation had proceeded he had dismissed the idea. He chose to think it was simply that Ulrich wanted him to get a wider perspective on life, so he'd contacted the people listed. But Inspector Lutzi's call now put a different complexion in things. Achille had instinctively kept the existence of the folder from the Inspector and now he had been found out.

From what Inspector Lutzi said, there had been at least four other people, apart from Mrs. Schmidt, with whom he'd had talks. None of them was listed on a page in the folder, so the five must be special in some other way? He then assumed the information must be in a deeper form of code, somehow hidden within the six sheets he'd been left, including Max's letter. If his surmise was correct, the hidden code was not one Achille could even begin to address? Why should he calmly hand them over to the Inspector. They were left to him personally, presumably for a reason?

Achille photocopied Ulrich's letter and ran-off the five sets of biblical quotations he'd translated including the names and locations of the people but not the dates. It was the oddity of the date he'd noticed on Leonard Osrow's sheet that caused him to instinctively withhold them all?

Achille did a covering letter to Inspector Lutzi, apologising once again. He didn't tell the Inspector he'd deciphered them from the originals left by Ulrich but that he had simply put everything on his computer. In that way he hoped to satisfy him and keep the existence of the original sheets secret.

Then Achille thought more about why Ulrich had chosen to leave them to him? What was he to do; it was for a reason he couldn't yet fathom? His mind was going round in circles. Then he remembered that Ulrich didn't say he'd copied the document that was pushed into his pocket that fateful Sunday. What he said was that he'd encoded it so that he could honestly deny making a copy, then burnt the original.

It was splitting hairs but it obviously mattered to Ulrich. Perhaps he, Achille, had subconsciously chosen to ignore the possibility of something like this because it seemed too far-fetched and potentially fraught with danger. But look where it had got him? He thought it was quite possible that Canon Zimmerman had told them about him. Thinking about the consequences made him really frightened."

Trying to be calm and rational, Achille felt that Ulrich didn't intend any danger to him but simply to act as he saw fit. He thought that as Ulrich probably worked for the British, he'd felt safe leaving the information in Achille's care, trusting he would pass what ever it was on to the British?

He didn't know how long his ploy with Inspector Lutzi would last or, more frighteningly, how soon the torturers would trace him, so felt that he had to act fast? He decided to phone the Foreign Office, to see if he could make an appointment with someone. He'd explain that he thought he might hold the key to some important secret?

His call didn't get him very far initially. Whoever answered the 'phone probably thought of him as some kind of crank. However, before he'd called, he'd worked out a way to convince the person taking his call. He told him about the three murders in Switzerland. Murders he was led to believe by the Swiss police that were as a result of ex-Nazis trying to obtain the information that was in his possession.

First there was Maureen Alcock, who'd worked as a multi-lingual secretary in our Swiss Embassy in Berne during the Second World War. She later married a Mr. Hoffman and was tortured and murdered in 1962. Her husband, who was in the Swiss Diplomatic Service then disappeared, changed his name to Max Sieber and suffered the same fate in 1978. Finally just five days ago, Max Seiber's best friend - Canon Zimmerman, of St. Ursen's Cathedral in Solothurn was tortured and died of a heart attack.

He went on to tell him the Hoffmans lived in Berne until Mrs. Hoffman was killed, then Mr. Hoffman lived as an eremite in Solothurn. Achille asked the man taking his call, to check these facts, via our Embassy, to establish his bona fide. He asked him not to contact the Swiss police as an Inspector Lutzi in Solothurn had questioned him on these matters and was possibly already close to recognising that he, Mr. Aarden, was holding the key.

Seven days later he got a phone-call at work, asking if he could come to London to see a Mr. Smith, the man with whom he'd previously spoken. Five days after that he was seated in a non-descript office with Mr. Smith and a Mr. Jones. They asked him to take them through the whole story in great detail. They asked questions for clarification as he went along. Finally Mr. Jones asked, "Did you bring the papers you say Mr. Hoffman left you?"

"Yes, well I've brought photocopies; I've deposited the originals at my bank."

117

"So, after three hours, Achille left with a promise that they would be in touch."

"It was some weeks before they got in touch, during which time Achille died a thousand deaths. As the time passed and with his absorption in work, the initial feeling of being vulnerable to capture, torture and even being killed, slowly wore off.

****

Sixteen

Dear Pascal,

Thanks for your letter and your description of Day One of creation. I have only two comments; I am really looking forward to reading days two to six and was intrigued at how you'd managed to phrase your description to use the actual words of Genesis.

Whilst writing I thought I'd draw your attention to three books you might be interested to read? I've picked them up over the last few months: Reading matter on my travels.

The first talks about time. Ulrich's 'Half-Life of Time' is echoed in a way, in a book by Alvin Toffler, published in 1970, which talks about the way time seems to be accelerating. It's called 'Future Shock'?

It made me think of Ulrich's idea as a kind of logarithmic progression? If one plots each of his thirty-three steps of time on logarithmic graph paper, then each point in time is in fact equidistant from the adjoining points. This enabled me to see clearly, albeit in a different way, how each step of time can be seen as being of the same length. That is, the amount that can be achieved through the advances made by mankind in previous steps, even though it passes in half the time. It simply depends on how one chooses to look at time. As I'm sure you know, Einstein proved that time is a variable dimension. Quite a fascinating subject?

The second book is called 'The Weather Book', published by M. Joseph Ltd. It talks about all kinds of weather patterns, including global warming, so I thought you might be interested to read it? It also talks about global cooling and the ice ages.

The third book is the most controversial of all. It's called 'Faster than the Speed of Light'. It's written by a Dr. Joao Magueijo and goes a long way to supporting Ulrich's contention that light can travel faster than it's present speed!

If you'd like to borrow any or all of them, I'd be happy to send them to you, just give me a call and consider it done.

My very kindest regards.

Achille

****

In the meantime, Herman Fritz, the secretary to be, was sent to Europe by Otto Altmann, Chairman of the Post War Finance Committee. He introduced himself to their Detective Agency team in Zurich and told them of the decision regarding Mr. Aarden, along with a number of other matters.

He met with some resistance to the idea of kidnapping and torturing Mr. Aarden in England. They did not speak good English, would probably stand out in an English environment and had already risked three killings in Switzerland. Doing something similar, away from home territory in England, would be far too risky.

A compromise was thrashed out. Having traced Mr. Aarden, they now knew he travelled to Europe frequently. They also knew what they were looking for, an A4 folder.

They would sub-contract breaking and entering into the Aarden home, to an agency that undertook such work. If that agency failed to find the relevant folder, then the team would kidnap Mr. Aarden on his next trip to Germany or Switzerland.

****

Seventeen

It was about two weeks later that Achille and Miriam's home was entered and searched. Miriam phoned Achille in some distress, about an hour before he planned to leave for home. She'd just got home from the office herself.

By this time, Olivia was travelling as a stewardess and Amber was away at university in her final year so the house had been empty. There was no sign of a forced entry to alert Miriam when she got home. She disarmed the security system as usual so it came as a complete shock when she saw the papers from the Canterbury thrown all over the sitting room floor. She looked round the rest of the house and saw there were papers everywhere all over the study and their bedroom. Achille told her not to start tidying-up. He'd come straight home.

Achille's immediate thought was how fortunate it was that he'd lodged Ulrich's folder at the bank. On the drive home he thought to himself, don't be so melodramatic, it's probably just plain robbery. Had anything been stolen like money for drugs or some of Miriam's jewellery? Then he realized his first thought was probably right. From what Miriam had explained, it was not a forced entry but was made with picked locks or duplicate keys. To de-activate the alarm indicated a high level of sophistication, a professional job. The clincher, to his mind, was that they seemed to have concentrated on papers.

When he got home, he and Miriam went from room to room, tidying up and trying to establish if anything had been stolen – it finally appeared not to be the case.

Achille had told Miriam about his meetings with Max Seiber and all that had followed since. She also knew about his visits to Max's other contacts and to Inspector Lutzi. She knew about Ulrich's papers and what Achille had done with them. She'd said his idea about possible Nazi activity and murder was too far fetched but when he approached the Foreign Office and they gave him an interview, it had given her food for thought. Achille had not told her about the recent torture and death of Canon Zimmerman, he didn't want to worry her although he was now very worried indeed. They would now be after him.

They decided to call the police, if for no other reason than to establish that a break-in had occurred for insurance purposes, in case something had been stolen which they might subsequently want to claim. They also decided that to raise the possibility of Nazi involvement would seem too far fetched. The Foreign Office were hopefully treating it seriously anyway,

The local police were not very helpful. They found it hard to believe their story. There was no forced entry, the alarm didn't go off, nothing was broken and, apparently, nothing was stolen. In fact, Achille and Miriam began to wonder if they thought they had staged it, having suddenly become attention seekers. They said they'd log it and left. Achille even wondered if their attitude was some kind of veiled threat to deter them from any such future ruse. They decided Achille would mention it as and when the Foreign Office contacted him.

The biggest surprise of Achille's life came five weeks after the break in. It had him mentally reeling for days afterwards. He had got a call from Mr. Smith asking if he could come up to London again. He and Mr. Jones would like to talk to him.

The meeting started with Mr. Jones saying "A great deal has happened since you came to see us so we'll deal with each item in chronological order as far as possible.

"First the copy papers from Mr. Hoffman you left with us. Let me say no more than we knew of Ulrich Hoffman and Maureen Alcock. Once this had been established from our records, we took what you told us seriously.

"After a preliminary scrutiny of the documents, we decided to pass them to our code breakers. A couple of the older members of that team recognized the five pages, excluding his letter, as probably a pentagonal code but with two significant variations which took time to resolve.

"Mr. Hoffman was both clever and difficult. The cleverness was in the biblical quotations that have no references, thus highlighting their importance. A biblical scholar was contacted who soon gave us the missing references, bar one. This was not in the bible at all although it did superficially appear to be so – this was the first breakthrough.

"Apparently and I know little about such matters, in a pentagonal code one needs to know the starting point from which to decipher the code, otherwise it is meaningless. The sequence of all five elements was given by the years on the dates of the documents and that was it.

"The second variation was his use of the simple telephone code and other variations. He had to play around with various simple codes to arrive at the particular numbers and letters he needed. This telephone code allows one a choice of three or four letters from the use of a single number. Conversely, any number from two to nine can be represented by any one of three or four letters. They got there in the end and, as Mr. Hoffman had surmised, it was indeed a Swiss bank security box number.

"We then got in touch with our Swiss counterparts and entered into preliminary negotiations to open the box. It became clear that Inspector Lutzi had approached them regarding Mr. Hoffman's role in their Diplomatic Service. The combination of his past activities and our approach proved to be a delicate subject upon which to tread.

"Your story was open to question until Inspector Lutzi stated that you are strangely unique, the only person he has so far met in whom Mr. Hoffman confided details of his earlier life. This fact, added to your story, your parentage, your overt contacts with Mrs. Schmidt, Canon Zimmerman, the Italian Ms Alessio, as well as the American and Frenchman, all helped to confirm your position in this matter – all this, combined with the photocopied documents, meant your *bona fides* were accepted.

"Incidentally, Inspector Lutzi bears no ill feelings, no grudge over your lack of candour. He understands your reluctance to tell all. Might I suggest that the next time you visit Solothurn you apologise in person and then take him to lunch?

"We proposed that an inventory be made of the contents of the accounts documented in the security box. Preliminary estimates put the value at between forty and fifty million pounds. Having established your right in this matter, we followed the outline of our earlier hypothetical discussions with you. We suggested that the disposition of the assets follow certain guidelines.

"We and the Swiss will jointly attempt to trace Jewish families and others who could have a valid claim to any of the contents. The cost of doing so to be covered from the sale of any residual assets but much will probably have to be returned to their rightful owners. For example there are two of Munch's oil paintings that might be worth a couple of million each. They will need to be returned to Norway, along with other plundered material that no doubt took place during the German occupation.

"We also suggested that the Swiss bank receive a commission on the saleable residue in recognition of their safekeeping of these assets over the last fifty or so years. The remainder of the money realized from the sale, to be split equally between the Catholic Church in Switzerland and we, the British.

"It has also been mooted that a sum is given you in recognition of bringing your secret to us, your friendship with Mr. Hoffman and his legacy to you – this is still the subject of some debate. It is being argued that by coming to us, we have probably been instrumental in avoiding your torture and death as well as avenging the death of your friend, his wife and Canon Zimmerman. Let me explain.

"Once we understood the positions held by Hoffman and Alcock and what happened to them and Canon Zimmerman, we thought you could also be in danger so we had you carefully watched. We immediately noticed that some other people were interested in you as well which indicated potential trouble and confirmed both our suspicions. From photos we took, we established that they were from a rather suspect private detective agency, here in London.

"We got in touch with our German and Swiss counterparts and learned that this agency had probably been sub-contracted to do the job by an agency owned and controlled by ex-Nazis that had recently met in Vienna. We then took great care to protect you and your family.

"We took telephoto-lens photographs of them entering and leaving your house. We did not arrest them because we wanted them to lead us to their employer, hopefully one or more of the ex-Naxi group.

"Excuse me but now I'll need to refer to a report from time to time, to relate the events that took place in Germany. We understand two of our people flew to Germany with you on one of your regular trips to Idstein, via Frankfurt. As I said, we'd already contacted Interpol so our men met two of our German counterparts at the airport. They identified two other men who were obviously expecting you. I know it sounds a bit like the Keystone Cops but our team followed them, following you.

"After you booked into the Nasser Hof in Wiesbaden, we kept a very close eye on them. They met up with a man who was obviously directing their activities. We photographed and identified him as the head of the Detective Agency in Zurich. This man had brought four others, two of whom were very nasty individuals, suspected of all kinds of mayhem. They no doubt established their plan of action that evening.

"After you met your business colleagues from around Europe and having overheard some of the conversation, we were pretty sure you'd stay in the hotel chatting business. However, we left two men in the hotel, in case you either went out, or they came for you in the hotel which we thought unlikely.

"Our German colleagues had requested the help of the local police to ensure we had sufficient manpower. After some discussion with them, we thought it likely they would try to take you in the morning on leaving the hotel or on the drive to Idstein.

"We had to let them make their move to ensure we had a charge on which to hold them, pending further enquiries. We planned to have four men at the hotel early in the morning to grab them if they made a move as you went to the car park but thought it more likely it would take place on one of the country roads rather than in the hotel or in town.

"We studied a map to decide the best location for the probable ambush; three routes were possible. The least likely would be the dual carriage way, east out of Wiesbaden to the E5 autobahn because it was the longest. The second was the 455 northeast to the E5, joining one junction further up the autobahn and third, the 417 country route north, turning right in the villages of Neuhof, to go northeast and passing under the E5 at the autobahn junction for Idstein. The 1.6Km from the E5 to Idstein was the only common denominator of which they could be absolutely sure. An early morning covert reconaissance confirmed that they had come to the same conclusion.

"To cut a long story short, our four men at the hotel followed you in two cars as you and your three colleagues drove cross-country.

You were lucky not to crash into the car that shot out of the autobahn exit for Idstein, blocking your path. As you saw for yourself, our armed response team emerged from hiding and levelled their guns at the men, once they got out of their cars and surrounded your car.

"Our men followed you and managed to sandwich one of their cars between our two unmarked police cars, effectively putting them out of action. The other car was just round the next bend to block traffic coming in the opposite direction. Our men were able to arrest all of them. It was all over in less than five minutes. You were able to proceed to the factory after our German colleagues apologized for the fright and short delay."

Achille said "My colleagues and I were shaken when we skidded to a halt when that car shot in front of us. We only just managed to stop. We wondered what was happening when the armed police surrounded us. We thought the police had probably been chasing crooks along the autobahn and the crooks decided to try and lose the police in the back streets of Idstein.

"Afterwards we thought that they stopped on a sudden impulse to capture us as hostages. That was nearer the truth than I care to think about as it was me they wanted. We could see round the bend in the road where your men had guns levelled. We saw men handcuffed and put into unmarked cards. Then everybody drove off, some driving the crooks' cars. We also wondered why we hadn't been delayed for statements and the like."

"Well, now you know. We've also arrested the two men who entered your house and they're being questioned. Two of the Germans that were arrested are now the subject of extradition proceedings between Germany and Switzerland. They are wanted for questioning in connection with the two murders in Berne and Solothurn and for manslaughter. Inspector Lutzi is sure he's gathered sufficient evidence from the scenes of crime to get a conviction."

"You've really shaken me," Achille said. "I hadn't realized what was going on. I did worry about what might happen but as time passed, the worry eased. After the events in Germany, I did wonder but as I hadn't heard from you, I dismissed the idea that they were connected. How wrong can one be? You've made me very thankful I decided to come to you but I never realized anything was happening until now."

Smith and Jones told Achille that it's government policy to keep knowledge of the existence of ex-Nazis confined to South America. "They don't want the public to know about their activities in Europe. That's why you weren't asked for statements.

"Rebuilding international relations across Europe, particularly with Germany, is thought to be too important to raise such issues that come from the aftermath of World War II. Incidentally, we'd like you to sign the Official Secrets Act document so don't tell anyone about what happened. It's just between ourselves. As I said, it never happened."

"I'll be happy to sign. You probably saved my life. That's the least I can do."

****

It was many years later that Olivia learned of the outcome.

The calculation of all the hidden accounts they'd found untouched in Switzerland was £43 million.

Tracing the ownership lasted a year but only £10 million pounds worth could be traced. The Swiss bank got their commission which came to a little under £3 million. The Catholic Church in Switzerland and the English government each received around £15 million.

The Swiss Church added it to a clergy retirement fund that they were building up because, up to that time, the clergy didn't get a pension. It helped to solve what was becoming an increasingly difficult problem. As vocations to the religious life declined, so did the number of convents and monasteries. The aged clergy had nowhere to retire to. The money was a godsend.

Achille never knew what the English Government did with their money but he was given an ex gratia payment of £50,000 in recognition of the fact that he was bequeathed the folder and chose to pass it to the Government.

****

Some time later Achille finally took Miriam to Switzerland for a long weekend to see Solothurn, St Ursen's Cathedral and the hermitage. Achille went to apologise to Inspector Lutzi. They took him to the very best restaurant in Solothurn for lunch. He told them all about the court case of the two Swiss nationals who were extradited and convicted on two counts of murder and one of manslaughter. They would be in prison for a very long time indeed.

****

Olivia speculated that it was this case, initiated by Ulrich, her father and the English government which probably triggered the secret and drawn out negotiations that culminated in the overt Swiss actions of 1997 and 1998. To quote:-

In 1997 Switzerland agreed to use its gold reserves in order to create a fund to help the victims of genocide, catastrophes and poverty and to compensate for the failure of some Swiss banks to return money to descendants of Jews who died in the Holocaust during World War II.

Further controversy had erupted over Switzerland's provision of financial services to Germany's Nazi government during World War II. Accusations were made that Switzerland had allowed German trains full of Jews and Italian slave labourers through its borders, en route to concentration camps. Additionally they cited its refusal of asylum to Jewish wartime refugees.

Facing what one diplomatic source described as Switzerland's worst foreign policy crisis since the war, some Swiss officials responded by denying that Switzerland had anything to apologise for, there were also reports of a rising incidence of anti-Semitism in Switzerland.

However, in August 1998, two major Swiss banks; Union Bank of Switzerland and Credit Suisse, agreed to pay US $1.25 billion to families of those who had suffered in the Holocaust.

In December 1998, Switzerland elected as their Federal President, Ruth Dreifuss, its first female President and, what is more, a Jewess.

****

Eighteen

Dear Mr. Aarden,

I heard about your near miss in Germany. You were rescued, it seems, in the nick of time. Two of the men captured are suspected of quite a number of unlawful activities but none as serious as our two murders and the manslaughter, so we took priority in the extradition process.

If you had told me about the folder and given it to me, we might never have apprehended the villains. I'm 90% sure, even at this stage, that they are the ones we have been trying to trace. One of the group also arrested, is in fact the head of a detective agency here in Zurich. He was in Vienna in 1979 when Interpol almost captured two ex-Nazis that had been at a secret meeting. The evidence is piling up and I'm 99.9% confident we will get convictions.

In light of all this I decided I would send you English summaries of the five interviews we conducted with the other Max visitors. One more came forward since the time we last spoke on that matter, I hope you find them of interest.

I'm glad you survived and if you come this way again I'd be pleased to see you and bring you up to date on the case.

Yours sincerely.
Inspector Lutzi.

Interviewee - Silvano Lucia - Locarno

He said that he'd asked the hermit whether he believed there are many more worlds in the universe with life on them, not just our world? The hermit's reply was along these lines: -

"I don't know if it will ever be proven one way or the other. But to think that we are the only beings in the universe is probably too egotistical. A bit like the Catholic Church excommunicating Copernicus at the time he had the audacity to suggest that the Earth revolved about the sun.

I doubt we will ever know, one way or the other. The distances in space are so vast that I think any radio transmissions, if they are at our power level, would be so attenuated as to be indistinguishable. The exception might be by the use of radio telescopes like that new one at Jodrel Bank. We've had radio for barely a hundred years; say we have it for another two thousand, that's still only one four-millionth of the age of the universe at the very most.

I think that worlds have probably formed and died before ours and the process will no doubt continue after ours has finished. But, in the vastness of time, for two civilisations, on two planets, to be at similar stages of radio capability at the same time and close enough to hear each other, would be an almost unbelievable coincidence.

I think this because in Mathew, Mark and Luke's gospels, when Jesus talks about the end of the world, he says, '... *before this generation has passed away all these things will have taken place.'* The end of the world didn't come before that generation had all passed away. So I concluded that when he said *'this generation',* what He meant was that this particular world of ours, as one of the planetary 'generations' in the universe."

Interviewee - Gertrude Cott – Liestal

Mrs. Cott had a discussion with Max Seiber in which the question of Christianity and all other religions became the subject of debate. Mr. Seiber said that most religions are based on belief in God and many live good lives as a result of their faith. He continued by saying that Christianity contains three key differences of faith to other religions, I wrote them down verbatim.

The first is based on God's teaching - in his first letter to the Thessalonians, St. Paul makes this point: - *"When we brought you God's message, you accepted it for what it really is God's message and not some human thinking."*

The second is contained in a conversation between Jesus and Nicodemus, as recorded in St. John's Gospel, when Jesus said, *God did not send His son into the world to be its judge but to be its saviour.*

The third point is that we believe that not only did Christ come to teach us, then suffered and died for His trouble at mankind's hands but also most importantly, that he rose from the dead. Jesus, in his story of 'The Rich Man and Lazarus' gave meaning to this in chapter sixteen of St. Luke's gospel. It ends: - *But Abraham said 'If they will not listen to Moses and the prophets, they will not be convinced even if someone were to rise from death.'*

This third point, His rising from the dead is the key element of our faith. In that same conversation with Nicodemus, Jesus also said - *Whoever believes in the Son is not judged; but whoever does not believe has already been judged, because he has not believed in God's only son.*

The discussion didn't last for very long but he gave Mrs. Cott a copy of a poem he'd written about Christ's passion and death (attached). He ended by saying, very few people in the world have not heard of Christianity - they have the freedom of choice, to accept or reject Christ's message.

The Last Supper ended - The Eucharist was born.
Gethsemane a walk - A prayer so forlorn.
This burden please lift - But Your will be done.
Betrayed by a kiss - Human race to be won.

To Caiaphas for silver- To Pilate for reproof.
A crown of thorns for silence - A scourging for the truth.
Our sins replaced with love - Yet like Peter we stand by,
Christ's innocence - sentenced - His punishment to die.

Mortified and tortured - Jesus condemned to die.
Christ bears our sinful burden - Tow'rd Calvary on high.
With a rough hewn cross - Borne on flesh scourged raw,
Suffering and staggering - To a death He foresaw.

The weight of the cross - With its splintered grain.
Weakness and blood-loss - Increases the pain.
The burden of sin - Committed by all.
A load so heavy - To stumble and fall.

Mary his mother - So brim-full of dread.
A sword through the soul - Simeon once said.
A meeting of love - Their very souls bared.
His mother, her son - Such deep sorrow shared.

Seeing His weakness - The cohorts proclaim,
Simon of Cyrene - Should carry some pain.
Forced into service - Became a labour of love,
Carrying the cross - With grace from above.

Midst an unruly crowd - That was baying for blood.
Veronica stepped forth - With compassion and love.
She wiped Christ's brow - Her motive so pure.
A miracle He worked - His countenance secure.

O Saviour sublime - 'Tis our sorrow to weep.
Your agony - our shame - A destiny you keep.
You fall yet again - For sins so severe.
Forgive us dear Lord - For bringing you here.

Watching the cruelty - His appearance obscene.
Wailing women He met - Who were viewing the scene.
 "Don't cry for Me - On this Calvary way,
But for your children" - He bade them to pray.

The hill seemed so steep - His steps far less sure.
Love's urgent struggle - His purpose so pure.
In living this agony - He could scarce bear the pain,
Our Christ weaker still - He fell yet again.

Cloth stuck to flesh - Blood setting, the glue.
Clothes stripped away - Some skin came too.
There naked He stood - His dignity gone.
Bared to crowd's view - But His true love shone.

Arms 'n legs outstretched - Prostrate on that truss.
Rough wood 'gain'st scourged back - You bore this for us.
Nails driven through flesh - Next' nerves, vein and bone.
The screaming of pain - As metal's banged home!
The cross then raised high - Increasing the pain.
Three nails took your weight - Arms 'n legs took the strain.
John, the Lord loved - Gave home to Christ's mother.
A notice wrote Pilate - Jewish king; none other!
Two thieves, left and right - One full of sorrow.
"You'll enter with me – My kingdom tomorrow."
The soldiers forgiven - "They know not what they do".
"All accomplished" said Christ - "God my spirit to you".
Sky dark, ground shaken - The spear's confirmation.
Our sins are forgiven - Our heart's desolation

Joseph asked Pilate - His permission obtained.
Taken down from the cross - These events pre-ordained.
Embraced by His mother - With sorrow so deep.
She could not comprehend - Only shudder and weep.

Desolation sore felt; -Apostles let down.
The end of a dream - No monarch's crown.
The disciples didn't know - The end of Christ's pain,
Being laid in the tomb - Was the start of His reign!

Mary Magdalene saw Christ - At dawn the third day.
John and Peter came rushing - Only shrouds where He lay?
Christ's rising does prove - Death has no sway.
His commands to follow - Is the true Christian way.

<u>Interviewee</u> - Maria Ananne - Porrentruy

Mrs. Ananne recalled her meeting with the hermit with ease; it had made a great impression on her. She had lived in

134

the village of Derendingen before she married, about two kilometres outside Solothurn. She was aware that a hermit lived on the outskirts of the town and met him one Friday lunchtime in September 1969, when they were both looking for a book.

They were looking for something on space travel after the Apollo eleven landing on the moon in July 1969. She was on her lunch break from the office, wanting to buy a birthday present for her fiancee: he wanting to learn more about space. They spoke about the possibility of space travel to the planets and beyond.

When the weather was good, she normally ate her sandwiches in the park adjoining Nordringstrasse, so he walked with her. He said the Apollo landing had triggered his memory of a passage from the book of Revelation: - *Then I saw a new heaven and a new earth. The first heaven and first earth disappeared...*

He then told her about something he'd already read; it was about the lead-up to the moon landing. That the seed of mankind's journey into space had been planted with the first successful liquid-fuelled rocket fired in 1926. Its first practical use came with its development as a weapon of war, used in 1944/5 and known as the V II.

A later rocket powered the first space mission, a man-made satellite, "Sputnik I", which was sent into orbit around the Earth in '57. It was not long before satellites of all kinds became the norm. After experiments with animals in space from '57 to '60, Russia put the first cosmonaut - Yuri Gagarin into space, in April '61. By December '68 America sent men into orbit round the Moon in `Apollo 8`. Then in July - `Apollo 11` had achieved the first manned landing. Thus the gestation period, from the first liquid-fuelled rocket, to the first manned landing on another celestial body, covered a brief period of just forty-three years.

He then told her that he believed the moon landing was

like the earliest voyage by man, like a journey across an ocean on earth, to explore what was on the other side. He said mankind will probably be running out of mineral resources by the end of the twenty-first century. It will then learn a very salutary lesson, coming to terms with severe resource restrictions. What she'd witnessed on TV was probably the first step in the solution, the mining of minerals from our solar system.

If mankind can get to the moon in just forty-three years of development, he will surely be able to mine from moons and planets by the middle of the next millennium at the latest, probably sooner.

Interviewee - Stefan Brevin - Zug

Mr. Brevin met Max Seiber in 1976 he thinks. He knows it was the year that the phrase 'Limits to Growth' was coined, when man first recognised the finite nature of the earth's resources. They discussed the use of energy from coal, gas, oil and nuclear.

The hermit had just finished reading a new book, 'Energy - The Solar-Hydrogen Alternative'. He thought it had great merit; it resonated with some of his own thinking. He'd often speculated as to whether mankind had travelled down the wrong path in harnessing carbon fuel? He'd concluded - probably not.

Mankind needed the industrial revolution to develop the technology he would require to adequately harness the power of the sun in all its forms, to meet mankind's voracious appetite for energy. He trusted in God - He had provided the fossil fuel. Through faith, he believed it was not sufficient for mankind to damage the planet permanently but enough to give it a fright and the time to learn how to harness alternatives?

The book had reassured him. Mankind was now in a position where it could begin to effectively harness the power of the sun, the heat of the deserts, the strength of the wind and the energy in the movement of the sea, to provide all its needs - a wholly natural solution. As psalm nineteen says: -

God made a home in the sky for the sun; it comes out in the morning like a happy bridegroom, like an athlete eager to run a race. It starts out at one end of the sky and goes across to the other. Nothing can hide from its heat.

A Cambridge lecture by Haldane in 1923, suggested that electricity could be generated from wind to produce hydrogen, via the electrolysis of water. Then liquefied, stored and distributed as a fuel.

The first really practical step came in 1933. A variety of men such as Errin, Hastings, Campbell and King all showed that an internal combustion engine could be run on hydrogen with only minor modifications.

Interviewee - Heinz Leibling - Langenthal

Being a farmer, when he met the hermit, he naturally asked what were his thoughts about agriculture. The hermit's first reaction was to quote from psalm 65. I made a note. It was verses 8 to 13, so I looked it up.

The whole world stands in awe of the great things that you have done. Your deeds bring shouts of joy from one end of the earth to the other. You show you care for the land by sending rain; you make it rich and fertile. You fill the streams with water; you provide the earth with crops. This is how you do it: you send abundant rain on the ploughed fields and soak them with water; you soften the soil with showers and cause the young plants to grow. What a rich harvest your goodness provides! Wherever you go there is plenty. The pastures are filled with flocks; the hillsides are full of joy. The fields are covered with sheep; the valleys are full of wheat. Everything shouts and sings for joy.

Mr. Leibling told the hermit that after World War II, the

scientific advances made, brought about a revolution in agricultural output. In 1955, once a degree of post-war stability had been established, agricultural output increased at an extraordinary pace. No aspect of farming was left untouched by the quiet revolution; improvement in one area often spun off into another.

The hermit's reaction was to say that he believed it could be God preparing adequate food supplies for the day when mankind suffers from a poorer climate and rising sea levels consuming agricultural land.

He thinks mankind's actions will so affect the natural order of things, that famine, on an unprecedented scale, will finally visit the earth but the advances in output will limit its scale. He quoted a second biblical passage (Jer: 14. 4 - 6) that foretells of this time; which I also looked up.

`Because there is no rain and the ground is dried up, the farmers are sick at heart; they hide their faces. In the fields. The mother deer abandons her newborn fawn because there is no grass. The wild donkeys stand on the hilltops and pant for breath like jackals; their eyesight fails them because they have no food.

Needless to say, Mr. Leibling found what the hermit had to say somewhat depressing.

****

Nineteen

There were various old gentlemen holidaying on the island of Curacao in a variety of hotels, some with wives, some with mistresses, one, secretly, with a male partner, some alone. Each had booked independently; simply ensuring they were on the island for a specified Thursday afternoon. Thus the Post War Finance Committee met at the Hilton in great secrecy for their 34th annual session in 1980.

Item 1 on the agenda was the election of the new secretary. Discussion between various members over the intervening year had made it a *fait accompli* - with Herman Fritz having already been sent to Europe. He was duly elected.

Before turning to item 2, the chairman, Otto Altmann informed the members that he wished to make a general statement.

"I am sorry for the inconvenience to members but security has had to be tightened. It transpired that the Vienna meeting was held with a false sense of security. Both our existence and the meeting had been compromised and two of us were very lucky to have avoided capture. We can no longer rely on our European detective agency for absolute security or, it would seem, for effectively carrying out our orders.

Our new secretary, Herman Fritz, will give you the details later but we lost two key members of our agency and six others. All are in prison awaiting trial on various charges; the two key operatives are the subjects of extradition proceedings to Switzerland on two counts of murder and one of manslaughter.

We have now cut all connections with the agency and none of the staff remain. We are in the process of setting up an entirely new cadre to be able to continue operations. Let me assure you once more, nothing and no one will remain that can lead back to us.

"...Now we come to item 5, the Hoffman deceit. Herman will bring us up to date."

"Well gentlemen, the old agency traced Mr. Aarden and searched his home, unsuccessfully, for the document passed to him by Canon Zimmerman. It was decided to capture him on one of his regular trips to his company's factory in Idstein. Security was once again compromised somewhere along the line because the two key members, Herr Altman referred to earlier and four others, were captured by an armed German police squad, moments before Mr. Aarden's capture.

"The two operatives, that were sub-contracted in England to search Mr. Aarden's house, were arrested at about the same time as the German operation was taking place - obviously by arrangement.

"The English and Swiss governments are in discussion over the release of the estimated £43 million, which we have been trying to trace for so many years. The two governments propose identifying ownership of the contents, so far as they are able, to enable restoration to their rightful owners and will presumably share the rest.

"The new cadre will arrange to follow any ownership

transfers and once the recipients are identified, the cadre team plan to recover as much of our losses as possible. I am informed that this could amount to about one third of the original figure.

"So all is not lost but I fear we will have to write-off the other two thirds. I will keep you informed."

"Thank you Herman, so now we come to item 6."

****

Twenty

Dear Achille,

Thanks for sending the books, I've read two so far, I've found them interesting. As you suggested, they go quite a way to supporting Ulrich's ideas.

As I told you when I phoned, I've not been idle, I've now completed days two to six of Creation in my expanded version of Genesis, chapter one. I was encouraged by what you and Leonard had to say, so I hope you find the rest interesting?

My kindest regards,

Pascal.

Day Two

It was four billion, one hundred and eleven million, four hundred and sixty-two thousand, five hundred and twenty-nine years BC at the start of Day Two.

Then God commanded "Let there be a dome to divide the water and to keep it in two separate places..."

The Earth contained an abundance of dissolved gasses; hydrogen, oxygen, nitrogen. Carbon dioxide predominated. They poured forth from the surface through the extensive volcanic activity that encircled the globe. The hydrogen burned in the oxygen, due to the heat of the red-hot magma from which it came and formed water vapour. This, with the two other gases, nitrogen and carbon dioxide, formed the bulk of an atmosphere that built around the Earth, retained by its gravity.

Over many millennia the heat of the Earth caused the water vapour to stay in the atmosphere as a gas until the Earth cooled sufficiently and atmospheric cooling allowed clouds to eventually form through condensation. The water vapour condensed on to the trillions of specks of dust thrown up by the volcanoes, those suspended by convection, too light to fall back to the surface of the Earth.

These clouds then shielded the surface of the Earth from direct sunlight, helping to accelerate the cooling process. The cloud layer built in thickness as did the water droplet size, finally becoming large enough for gravity to cause rain to fall. This was, finally, the separation of water in cloud form above the Earth, from the rainwater building up on the surface below... *and it was done.*

So God had *made a dome* of what we call atmosphere and clouds above the Earth and *it separated the water under it from the water above it. He named the dome "Sky".*

Volcanism continued to encircle the Earth. The molten core bursting forth, spewing out millions upon millions of tons of material, this, in addition to the gasses that continued to build the atmosphere, clouds and rain. The sky, as a result, was permanently covered in cloud and laden with dust.

This continued to attenuate the sunlight falling on the surface of the Earth. As the Earth continued to cool - the water vapour condensed more quickly, the formation of clouds accelerated, thus producing ever more rain. It became a quickening spiral of meteorological activity that caused water to build upon the surface of the Earth, progressively covering it in an ever-deepening layer. Some water evaporated, adding to the cyclical pattern

As the Earth's cooling continued, more of the magma solidified into rocks, the oldest of these has been found in Greenland. It's a conglomerate rock, now commonly associated with a beach or a riverbed, dated at three point eight billion years old. The combination of volcanism and cooling caused a great mix of elements and many combinations to be randomly trapped within the thickening crust and atmosphere of the Earth. From hydrogen to fluorine, neon to argon - potassium to cobalt - nickel to krypton - rubidium to rhodium - palladium to xenon - caesium to europium - gadolinium to hafnium - tantalum to thallium - lead to thorium - protactinium and uranium. All ninety-two elements of the periodic table were present to a greater or lesser degree.

When this thickening crust became more rigid, averaging about eight miles thick at this time, it cracked into a series of what we now call tectonic plates. This was due to continuous distortion from the force of gravity exerted by the sun, moon and planets, as well as the magma's continued turmoil within.

God was not in a hurry, another two billion, fifty-five million, seven hundred and twenty-nine thousand, four hundred and nine years had passed - half of all remaining time. *Evening passed and morning came - that was the second day.*

Day Three

Then God commanded "Let the water below the sky come together in one place, so that land will appear."

Now had come the time in God's plan of creation, when evolution began to shape the surface of the world. Huge plumes of magma within the Earth and the pull of moon, planets and sun, lifted the broken crust in some areas, causing other areas to sink. The water drained away from the higher to the lower ground.

Thus some of the earth's surface rose out of the water that had covered the globe. The first of these was "Gondwanaland". It grew to be huge, covering a major part of the Southern Hemisphere. It was destined to be Antarctica, Australasia, South America, Africa and India.

A second area of land emerged -"Laurentia"- that also grew over time as the water drained away; this was in a mainly equatorial position. It was smaller than "Gondwanaland" and was to become North America, Greenland and Scotland.

Then a third area of land became exposed - "Siberia" - it sat astride the equator, on the opposite side of the globe. It became large and was destined to be most of Asia and part of Europe.

Finally a fourth, smaller area of land arose - "Baltica" - it would become the other part of Asia and the northern part of Europe.

As these four continents developed, some trapped inland waters remained. Volcanoes grew mountains and hills; their ash still filled the sky. It continued raining so rivers of water flowed in the warmer climes but glaciers formed in colder climes, each carving-out the land spectacularly.

These landmasses moved over time - continental drift - an inch or two each year, about a mile every sixty thousand years. This movement slowly took Gondwanaland northward, bringing what were to be Africa and South America towards the equator. Laurentia drifted southeast and Siberia drifted southwest; they eventually merged. One billion and twenty-seven million, eight hundred and fifty-two thousand, eight hundred and forty-nine years later - *and it was done.*

He named the land "Earth" and the water, which came together, he named "Sea". And God was pleased with what he saw.

Then God commanded "Let the earth produce all kinds of plants, those that bear grain and those that bear fruit."

The pre-requisites for plant growth were present. Water had covered and soaked the Earth's surface since the end of the Archezoic Period. There was a high concentration of carbon dioxide in the atmosphere for the plants to breathe. The humidity was high from excess water vapour that still formed clouds, still producing rain. Nutrients were present in

145

the earth, laid down over millions of years, produced by microfossils and a combination of bacteria as well as blue/green algae that thrived in warm shallow waters.

The trigger for the development of plants was produced by a massive burst of radiation from a super-nova. It caused a mutation, an aberration in the form of Eukarotes, a highly organised cell nucleus, surrounded by a membrane. They became the earliest forms of fungi and seaweed.

The Eukarotes contained chlorophyll and other pigments, allowing photosynthesis to gently take place in the very overcast and gloomy light. They lacked stems, roots or leaves but were the progenitors of today's plants.

In a very small way, the slow but steady consumption of atmospheric carbon dioxide started, aiding the building process of early forms of plant life. In turn, through the photosynthetic process, the plants released oxygen. In this way a slow transition of our atmosphere began, carbon dioxide being replaced by oxygen. The earth had started to awaken to the heavily filtered sunlight as the still crude Earth continued to creep towards the Cambrian Period of the Palaeozoic era. *So the earth produced all kinds of plants and God was pleased with what he saw.*

Another half of all remaining time had passed - one billion, twenty-seven million, eight hundred and fifty-two thousand, six hundred and forty-nine years. *Evening passed and morning came - that was the third day.*

Day Four

Then God commanded "Let lights appear in the sky to separate day from night and show the time when days, seasons and years begin; they will shine in the sky to give light to the earth"

Volcanism slowly declined. This caused a corresponding reduction in atmospheric pollution. The release of hydrogen, oxygen and other gasses was also declining. The atmosphere was beginning to approach a state of equilibrium, the heavy overcast conditions lightened progressively and the rains helped clear the sky of dust.

The total cloud cover began to break, revealing the sun, the moon and the stars to the surface of the Earth. At the same time the sun was growing hotter, creating near tropical conditions and the new light level accelerating the photosynthesis of plant growth.

A greater differential between land and sea temperature developed, caused by direct sunlight, in turn producing stronger thermals and more powerful winds. These two factors mixing the atmospheric gasses and creating more rapid evaporation altered the level of atmospheric instability. Consequently more variable meteorological cycles developed - Cumulo-Nimbus clouds formed more rapidly, followed by periods of heavy rain that watered the plants. The growth of plant life accelerated to become dense accumulations of single cell planktonic algae and multi-cellular phytoplankton, such as acritarchs. This sequence of meteorological activity continued throughout the Cambrian Period - *and it was done.*

So God made the two larger lights appear on Earth, *the sun to rule over the day and the moon to rule over the night;* he had *also made the stars* appear. *He* had *placed the lights in the sky to shine on the earth, to rule over the day and the night and to separate light from darkness.*

Meanwhile continental drift had continued to move Gondwanaland, Laurentia, Baltica and Siberia and they began to drift apart. By the end of this, the Fourth Day, all four would sit astride the equator. The tropical conditions combined with monsoon rains partly flooded the continents, the excess run-off water from melting glaciers producing an overall rise in sea levels. Some regional and localised uplifting of lands followed, caused by volcanic, mountain building activity, at the rim of the continental plates.

Some of these were the last of the super-volcanoes, which had filled the sky with dust; they have left traces, some of which have since been identified. The Long Valley Caldera in California, the Valles Caldera in New Mexico, the Kamchatka Caldera in Eastern Russia and the Yellowstone Caldera in Wyoming, to name but four.

A period of five hundred and thirteen million, nine hundred and twenty-nine thousand, five hundred and twenty-one years had passed, yet another half of all remaining time. God's commands were all growing to maturity. *And God was pleased with what he saw. Evening passed and morning came - that was the fourth day.*

Day Five

Then God commanded "Let the water be filled with many kinds of living beings and let the air be filled with many birds"

Protists, that is unicellular organisms that were on the borderline of plants, had formed and the first coelenterates had also evolved by the beginning of the Ordovacian Period.

Now came another tremendous burst of adaptive radiation, mutating the protists and coelenterates into a range of highly diversified trilobites, lampshells, graptolites and groups of gastropods. This adaptive radiation also brought into being sea urchins and was the origin of all five orders of starfish.

Then came a significant alteration to the evolutionary direction when the earth passed through the radiation belt of a Supernova, the result of an enormous cosmic explosion. It caused the mass extinction of much marine life, a seemingly random process that changed the direction of evolution.

As a result, the Silurian period saw the first jawed fishes appear - eurypterids, chondrichthyans and osteichthyans. The coral reefs that had built-up over aeons of time resulted in the formation of warm lagoons - in these, ammonites and the first amphibian tetrapods now evolved.

During the Devonian period, a second culling of marine life occurred from a further exposure to cosmic radiation, re-directing the evolutionary path yet again. 'Tiktaalik Roseae' emerged three hundred and seventy five million years ago, the first fish to exhibit signs of 'legs, the first fish to crawl onto land. After that came the first of the reptiles. Graptolites became extinct but early sharks and bony fish started to thrive. Trilobites finally died out and the early reptiles started to diversify, one being the progenitor of archaeopteryx, the first of the bird-like creatures. Other reptiles were the forefathers of the dinosaurs that were to appear in the Triassic Period.

So God created the great sea monsters and all kinds of creatures that live in the water and all kinds of birds. And God was pleased with what he saw. He blessed them all and told the creatures that live in the water to reproduce and to fill the sea and he told the birds to increase in number.

The same adaptive radiation had also caused plant life to diversify. First were spores, resembling those of modern plants. Then, in the Silurian Period, the first vascular plants started to grow - plants such as club mosses as well as yellow-green algae. There was progressive colonisation of the land by these plants and they became as big as today's trees. Ferns and then the first seeded plants, also began to appear.

Plant life became extremely verdant during the Carboniferous Period, producing many millions of generations of plants, over millions of years. The deposits from this vegetation formed into anthracite in the lowland swaps during the Jurassic Period. This fantastic growth of vegetation slowed as the proportion of carbon dioxide in the atmosphere diminished, coming closer to today's level, replaced by the increase in oxygen. The decaying plant material went on to produce bituminous coal, lignite and late in the period, brown coal and peat. During the process of decomposition, the vegetation also produced huge pockets of methane gas.

Then modern families of conifers, except pines, came into being and thrived in the drier conditions. Gymnosperm grew to dominance in the Triassic Period and ferns remained important. Forests of cycads, conifers and ginkoes spread ever further across the lands. That second burst of adaptive radiation also brought about a further change in vegetation. Deciduous and broad-leaved trees appeared and came to dominate many areas of land, also the first grasses appeared.

As fish and plant life evolved, so did the landmasses of the world. Baltica moved towards the equator, closer to Laurentia. On the other hand, the continent of Gondwanaland moved south and became much colder, causing glaciers to form once again. Some of these grew to within thirty degrees of the equator; they became so widespread that they caused the overall sea level to fall once more. Baltica finally collided with Laurentia to form a landmass called Laurasia.

The gap between Laurasia and Gondwanaland narrowed, the continental drift of the landmasses and the progressive warming of the seas, began to have a further climatic effect through the development of ocean currents. Finally, in the late Carboniferous Period and early Permian Period Laurasia and Gondwanaland finally collided to form the super-continent of Pangaea. Siberia subsequently collided with Pangaea, which started the formation of the Ural Mountains late in the Permian Period.

At the start of the Triassic Period almost all of the earth's landmasses were joined together. This huge landmass virtually covered one side of the world. The result was very arid conditions for large areas of the land that were far from water. The great ocean of Panthalassa covered the rest of the globe.

There were profound climatic differences from region to region but, as time passed, the world warmed once more, causing the heavy glaciation in the south to slowly melt, ocean levels rose again.

Yet again, half of all the remaining time had passed, another two hundred and fifty-six million, nine hundred and sixty-two thousand, eight hundred and fifty-seven years.

Evening passed and morning came - that was the fifth day.

Day Six

The Sixth Day of creation was markedly different. It was a day that lasted through fifteen steps of time - two hundred and fifty-six million, nine hundred and fifty-eight thousand, nine hundred and thirty-one years.

The first six steps covered the Triassic Period to the Pliocene Epoch. God intervened in three of the steps to ensure that evolution produced the kind of animal He wanted us to be - a particular form of animal that became humankind.

Once humankind existed, the second phase of Day Six covered nine further, ever quickening steps of time, making a total of twenty steps since the beginning of time. God acted on four more occasions to ensure that the evolution of humankind met His purpose, the point at which He could create Mankind.

Step Six of time was perhaps the most dramatic, it started at the transition from the Permian to the Triassic Period. It saw the greatest mass extinction of all time, around two hundred and fifty million years ago. Literally a seismic event, its magnitude so great it caused the extinction of 90% of all living creatures. It's now known as 'The Time of Great Dying'.

Its cause was a huge asteroid impact. It produced a massive crater, one hundred and twenty-five miles in diameter, called the 'Bedout High'. It hit an area just off the coast of southern Pangea, an area that is now off the northwest coast of Australia. The asteroid impact was so massive, it caused a ripple effect in the Earth's crust creating massive volcanic activity and opening up large pockets of methane gas. The atmosphere filled with both methane and debris, the sun dimmed, vegetation declined dramatically, the gas poisoned the atmosphere for both fauna and flora. The fittest 10% survived - the selected few heralded a major change in the direction of evolution once more.

Teleosts came into being, as well as the dominant fish groups of today and enormous marine reptiles such as ichthyosaurs and plesiosaurs. Thecodonts became the flying reptiles known as pterosaurs. The era of the dinosaurs emerged. Turtles, marine lizards and crocodiles that had been thriving declined significantly during the Jurassic Period. Dinosaurs diversified to the point where archaeopteryx, the first true bird-like creature appeared. It had well-developed wings and a body covered with feathers. Teleosts also underwent a dramatic change, producing herrings, carp, eels, cod and perch; they all thrived during the Cretaceous Period. In addition the most spectacular vertebrates appeared - marine plesiosaurs, giant turtles and the newly evolved Mosasaurs. The sea creatures, commanded on day five, were now a reality.

The penultimate moves that created today's geography were also taking place. Rifting occurred between Laurasia and Gondwanaland, initially separating Southern Europe from Africa. Pangea tore in two, opening up what is now the Central Atlantic. South America started to separate from Africa to begin to form the South Atlantic. What was to become India separated from Antarctica. Then the final phase began when Greenland tore away from the North American and European parts of Pangea.

One hundred and twenty-eight million, four hundred and seventy-nine thousand, five hundred and twenty-five years had passed. It was another half-life of time.

Then God commanded "Let the earth produce all kinds of animal life: domestic and wild, large and small"- this command began Step Seven of time.

The cataclysmic event in step six led the chosen genes into producing the coelacanth early in this step. It was part fish, part animal; it formed the next stage in the evolutionary transition from fish to animals.

With food in the form of plants, now available, the very first of the mammalian groups now emerged in the form of an early lemur like primate - Adapidae - evolution had produced the first step in the animal kingdom that would eventually lead to humankind - *and it was done.*

During this time, rifting in the Jurassic Period separated Europe from Africa, Iberia was left in between, this then started to converge on Europe.

Sub-tropical flora came as far north as present day Southern England.

Modern families of flowering plants evolved and the Palaeocene Epoch saw the emergence of today's grasses.

As Step Seven was drawing to a close, some sixty-four million years ago, a second cataclysmic event occurred. It was of lesser proportions than that which came earlier but none-the-less it caused the extinction of about 60% of all living creatures on Earth, including the dinosaurs. It was caused by another asteroid or large meteor impact in Chicxulub, an area off Mexico's Yucatan Peninsula. It produced a super-sonic shock wave that circled the Earth and brought about similar effects to that of the Bedout High impact, albeit less severe.

Step Seven of time lasted sixty four million, two hundred and thirty-seven thousand, eight hundred and sixty-one years. The first of the land animals had been created and another half of remaining time had passed.

The Eighth Step saw the pace of animal development and

diversity began to quicken. Hoofed animal groups evolved, early pigs, hippopotami, camels, deer and antelopes. Then came cattle, horses, tapirs and rhinoceroses. Anteaters, sloths, armadillos, elephants, whales and rodents followed. Early carnivorous animals then evolved such as cats, dogs, bears, racoons, hyenas, civets and weasels. Finally dwarf lemurs and aye-ayes that were squirrel-like lemurs emerged.

The Oligocene and Eocene Epochs saw the present range of trees emerge, which began to give the land a distinctly modern appearance. The continued development of grasses enabled them to invade open country and withstand heavy grazing.

The Indian tectonic plate had continued its journey northward and now began its collision with Eurasia, as the latter was then called, leading to the formation of the Himalayas over the ensuing 30 million years. The Eurasian Basin in the Far East began to open-up through the fragmentation at that end of the continent.

Iberia finally collided with Europe to begin the formation of the Pyrenean Mountains over the following 20 million years and Australasia separated from both South America and the Antarctic continent.

A further thirty-two million, one hundred and seventeen thousand, two hundred and twenty-nine years had passed, yet another half of remaining time.

Step Nine saw the start of God's final preparation to produce that special kind of animal, by means of the irradiation of mammals from another super nova.

Tarsiformes then emerged, looking like a lemuroid kind of monkey. These evolved into Tarsiers, a nocturnal primate with huge eyes, long hind legs and digits ending in pads to facilitate climbing. Anthropoids appeared that were early higher primates called Sakis. Further animal evolution brought into being Marmosets and Tamarins - monkeys with clawed digits and Gibbons, which were small agile anthropoid apes.

Owls and spiders also appeared and all orders of birds were now completed.

The climate deteriorated, the Polar Regions cooled. Significantly, less rain fell and by the end of the Oligocene Epoch glaciation had once more caused sea levels to drop appreciably. Forests shrank but herbaceous plants appeared and grasses continued to spread, becoming hardier.

The main phase of Alpine Mountain building began and rifting started in Northeast Africa, this was the first hesitant step that ultimately led to the formation of Arabia, the Red Sea and the Persian Gulf.

The Himalayas rose higher as India continued to push further into Asia. Then further movement in the tectonic plates along the rest of North Africa brought progress in the formation of the Mediterranean, it began to look like the sea we know today.

This Ninth Step of time took sixteen million, fifty-six thousand, eight hundred and thirteen years, yet another half of all remaining time.

Step Ten of time saw the emergence of yet more new animal groups including frogs, snakes, mice and rats.

Flora developed to the point where it looked much as today.

The uplifting of the Isthmus of Panama began. It would eventually bridge the gap between north and South America and finally separate the Atlantic and Pacific Oceans.

Whilst little seemed to have happened, it emphasised the length of time such events consumed, it brought some of the final touches, the refining of this phase of evolution. It lasted eight million, twenty thousand, six hundred and five years; once again it was half of remaining time.

Step Eleven was the end of this first phase of Day Six, lasting four million, eleven thousand, five hundred and one years. It was the consolidation of God's earlier commands to create the flora and fauna needed to support what was to come. 'Chad Tomah' emerged, the immediate forebear of the Hominids. Earth was ready for the final phase in His plan of creation.

The Isthmus of Panama was completed, joining North and South America. The sea levels started to rise again as the Earth warmed and ice melted. The geography of the world, its continents, oceans and seas, as well as all the Flora and Fauna was now as we know them today.

So God had *made them all and he was pleased with what he saw.*

So *then,* in Step Twelve, *God said "and now we will make human beings; they will be like us and resemble us. They will have power over the fish, the birds and all the animals, domestic and wild, large and small."* (Notice He said, *we will make human beings* - He didn't command; nor did He say 'we will make mankind'.)

The higher primates, Orang-utan, Chimpanzee, Gorillas and Gibbons followed from this intention. From these emerged the first generation of Hominids, Australopithecus, about three million four hundred thousand years ago. *So God created human beings making them to become like himself.*

It took a further two million, three thousand nine hundred and forty-nine years to produce humankind, another half of all remaining time.

The Thirteenth Step of time, this final sequence of evolutionary progress, saw an increase in brain size among the Hominids. This was the key to the further development of humankind - Hominoidea as he was called. Homo Erectus evolved from this predecessor, about one million, six hundred thousand years ago.

Then a very different and dramatic event occurred around one million four hundred and twenty thousand years ago when Homo Erectus learned to make and use fire. Humankind was, by then, firmly established on Earth and was beginning to use that extra brainpower to move beyond just needing food and sleep.

The end of Step Thirteen was also the end of the Pleistocene Epoch. Another one million, one hundred and seventy-three years had passed - yet another half of remaining time.

By the time Step Fourteen arrived there had already been some eighteen cold periods in the life of the earth - six had been quite severe. Now, four further ice ages came upon the Earth in 'quick' succession. The first of these, the Gunz ice age, occurred about eight hundred thousand years ago. This brought severe hardship to Homo Erectus, causing the demise of the majority and the survival of the few - the fittest. They were being progressively forced to move closer to the equator as the ice spread from the poles.

Another four hundred and ninety-eight thousand, two hundred and eighty-five years passed - the ever-quickening half-life of time.

The second ice age, the Mindel, came in Step Fifteen, about four hundred thousand years ago. It brought a further thinning-out of humankind; again it was the survival of the fittest, those most able to cope.

Another two hundred and forty-seven thousand, three hundred and forty-one years had passed. The ice age forced Homo Erectus to use his brain as well as his physical ability, to survive. Homo- Erectus was evolving and gaining in intellect. The interval between the ice ages allowed for a recovery in the population size, bred from this improved stock.

The Riss ice age came in Step Sixteen, about two hundred thousand years ago. It was a repeat of the process of humankind's brain and body development. It also produced a key genetic mutation, the FOXp2 gene that was to give humankind their unique speech capability.

This further half-life of remaining time took one hundred and twenty-one thousand, eight hundred and sixty-nine years.

The culling process caused by these ice ages had brought about very considerable development of humankind. A consolidation period was now provided for in Step Seventeen, a physical expansion and maturing of the Homo Erectus population.

It was a time for humankind to develop its newfound skills, further improve its ability to adapt to its surroundings and eventually become master of the fish, the birds and all the wild animals.

It consumed another half-life of remaining time, fifty-nine thousand, one hundred and thirty-three years.

At the beginning of Step Eighteen, it is estimated that some ten thousand pairs of Homo Erectus were spread across central Africa. They were the offspring of those who had elected to stay in, or move towards the warmer equatorial regions as the ice ages had spread from the poles. Of the remainder who had chosen not to migrate down into central Africa, the majority had died but a significant minority had survived. The severe conditions forced this latter group to become mentally and physically stronger. Their physical stamina and their survival skills were significantly superior.

The many generations that followed from the ice-age survivors became, to varying degrees, a very high order of animal indeed. They were far better placed to face the last ice age, the Wurm, about thirty one thousand years ago. It tested, developed and culled humankind one last time, producing the finalised stock of humankind. Homo Erectus became transformed into modern humankind - Homo Sapiens - about thirty thousand years ago.

He created them male and female, blessed them and said, "Have many children, so that your descendants will live all over the earth and bring it under control. I am putting you in charge of the fish, the birds and all the wild animals. I have provided all kinds of grain and all kinds of fruit for you to eat; but for all the wild animals and for all the birds I have provided grass and leafy plants for food"- and it was done.

Step Eighteen ended twenty-seven thousand, four hundred and fifty-three years BC. Another half-life of time had passed.

During Step Nineteen the Wurm ice age receded as the earth warmed once more, Homo Sapiens spread through Kenya, Ethiopia and Egypt into the eastern Mediterranean. They later continued on into Persia and across southern Asia as far as the Indian sub-continent.

Homo Sapiens was still corporeal, as had been the Hominids and Homo Erectus before them but now they began to show signs of creativity in the form of carvings and crude art decorating their cave dwellings, some dating back twenty-eight thousand years.

This all took place over a period of fifteen thousand, six hundred and eighty-four years; it was now 11,769 BC.

The Twentieth and final Step of Day Six, commenced in 11,769 BC and lasted until 3,927 BC, a further seven thousand, eight hundred and forty three years.

Homo Sapiens progressively became more social, language was evolving and they learned to farm and hunt in-groups. Around 9,000 BC, they had started to live in small communities, farmsteads, hamlets and villages. Evidence of permanent settlements have been found in the Near East and North Africa. There is also evidence of the domestication of animals as well as the growing of wheat and barley. In the thousand years 8,350 BC - 7,350 BC, Jericho, the first walled town in the world, was slowly built up.

Homo Sapiens had by now, migrated as far as China, where there is evidence that rice cultivation started around 7,250 BC. Anthropologists have also found traces of experiments made with copper ore in Anatolia around 7,000 BC.

Homo Sapiens was farming in Greece and the Aegean c.6,500 BC and a second city - Catal Huyuk - was built in Turkey, around 6,250 - 5,400 BC, where the first samples of pottery and woollens have been discovered.

Homo Sapiens spread up the Danube into Hungary, c.5,500 BC and along the Mediterranean coast to France, c.5,000 BC. They colonised the alluvial plains of Mesopotamia, practiced irrigation and formed agricultural settlements in Egypt around the same time. The migration continued into Germany, the Low Countries and Britain c. 4,500 BC.

Due to climate change, desiccation of the Sahara began c.4,000 BC. It divided the residual North African population in two, some were driven north, inhabiting the Mediterranean coast, whilst others moved progressively south once more.

In the last year of Step Twenty, or if one prefers, the first year of Step Twenty-one - 3,927 BC - there came the moment that God had chosen to create Mankind... *he breathed life-giving breath into his nostrils and the man began to live.*

This was the gift of a spiritual principle to human beings. The human body sharing in the dignity of "the image of God". A human body animated by a soul. A creation that signifies that mankind was and is enabled to have a spiritual dimension to share with God if he so chooses.

Mankind had, for the very first time, an awareness of the existence of God. A later chapter of Genesis looks back on this event, saying, *He created them male and female, blessed them and named them "Mankind".*

They were no longer simply human: They now had a

conscience as a result of having a soul. They could determine right from wrong, in addition to their power of logical and original thought. They had the ability to choose the path they would follow: They could think, plan and decide their own destiny.

They would gain dominion over the whole world: Mankind's horizons would become almost limitless. Mankind was no longer just a sophisticated animal, no longer corporeal, mankind was now able to live, not just exist!

God added, *"This is the beginning of what they are going to do. Soon they will be able to do anything they want!*

After two hundred and fifty-six million, nine hundred and sixty-two thousand, eight hundred and fifty-seven years of Day Six - the whole of creation was complete.

God looked at everything he had made and he was very pleased. Evening passed and morning came - that was the sixth day.

And so the whole universe was completed. By the seventh day God finished what he had been doing and stopped working. He blessed the seventh day and set it apart as a special day, because by that day he had completed his creation and stopped working. And that is how the universe was created.

****

From the moment when God chose to create the universe by means of a Singularity - eight billion, two hundred and twenty-two million, nine hundred and twenty-eight thousand seven hundred and sixty nine years BC, just over 99.9% of all time has passed for this world. Around one four millionth of it remained!

So it came to pass that Adam & Eve were recorded as the

161

first of mankind. They entered the Twenty-First Step of time which lasted from their creation in 3,927 BC through to 6 BC. The thirty-nine books of the Old Testament, from the remainder of Genesis to the prophet Malachi, tell about the earlier life of mankind, in all its colourful detail. In all sixty-one generations, ten from Adam and Eve to Noah, nine from Noah to Abraham and in the first chapter of St. Mathew's Gospel is listed the forty-two generations from Abraham to the birth of Christ.

6 BC was the year Christ was born - the beginning of the twenty-second step of time. The twenty-seven books of the New Testament, from St. Mathew's gospel to the book of Revelation, relate how God chose to educate mankind to enable it to share His greatest gift - heaven.

****

Dear Achille,

I thought I would add a note. I hope you found what I've written lives up to the standard of Ulrich's thinking and the main elements he discussed with Leonard.

What I really wanted to add concerns the complication I found when completing Ulrich's idea of the thirty-three steps of time. There was the fact that our calendar changes from BC to AD. The fact that Christ was born in 6 BC, according to biblical scholars, mentioned in a note at the end of the chart of biblical history at the back of the bible. And finally the fact that I had to round up or down, the decimal places in the AD years. This latter point illustrates that our calculation of time is not God's: We can never know therefore when the end of the world will come.

For the sake of completeness however, these are my attempt at defining the further twelve steps of time: -

162

Step 22   6 BC - 1955 AD
23   1955 - 2934
24   2934 - 3424
25   3424 - 3669
26   3669 - 3791
27   3791 - 3852
28   3852 - 3883
29   3883 - 3898
30   3898 - 3906
31   3906 - 3910
32   3910 - 3912
33   3912 - 3913

Yours once again

Pascal

****

Twenty-one

Achille learned of the death of his mother, from his daily 'phone call to Miriam, whilst on a visit to his company's head office in America. She was seventy-eight.

On his return, he chose to go back to the parish where his mother had met his father, in the Diocese of Westminster where they, as well as he and his sisters had been married. He was motivated by the fact that his mother could then be buried in the same grave as his father and paternal grandmother.

Meeting the parish priest was the most tremendous shock for Achille. It was none other than Father Walton! It was Alan, his close friend at St. Edmund's College who had continued through to the priesthood. They'd lost touch after Achille left.

Father Walton was intrigued by the story Achille told of how his mother came to England, met and married his father in his church and that he and his three sisters had also married there. He went so far as to look them all up in the parish register.

During their discussions of all the arrangements, Father Walton sensed Achille's discomfort. Relaxing in Alan's company, Achille felt he could finally reveal that he'd been a lapsed Catholic for some thirty years. He also admitted that he'd left and divorced his first wife and re-married in a Registry Office. Father Alan was not shocked but sympathetic, recognising Achille spiritual distress.

After the visit Achille wondered at how easily and suddenly, he'd unburdened himself to his schoolboy friend? He'd recognised a sympathetic ear in Alan.

Achille and Miriam, along with his three sisters, Anna, Emma, Eileen and their husbands, were at the Requiem Mass. It was at the usual hour of daily mass, so a number of parishioners were also present. Father Walton seemed to go out of his way to make the ceremony as meaningful and memorable as possible. He even told the parishioners, during a short address after reading the Gospel, how Mrs Arden had met and married her husband at this church and that the four children of the marriage, who were present, had also been married here. He went on to mention that one of them, her son, had been his close friend at school in their teenage years and how they were both surprised to meet up again after losing touch.

After the internment, the eight of them had lunched together, the first time this had occurred. They had lived their separate lives, brought up their children and had met many times at various baptisms and weddings but the eight of them together made this particular occasion unique. They found they enjoyed each others company to such a degree that they repeated it many times in later years.

The whole experience of his mother's death, burial and meeting Alan Walton as a priest, was cathartic for Achille. Since his first meeting with Ulrich and all that followed, particularly his close encounter with a bunch of ex-Nazis, the pressure within him, spiritually speaking had inexorably built. He felt that he wanted to go back to Alan to talk about it all, using him as his spiritual advisor, one whom he could trust, who already knew about him and his past.

He 'phoned Alan who knew that the loss of ones mother sometimes has a dramatic effect on those who have lapsed. What Father Walton didn't know, was how Achille's original wish to be a priest fell apart and more particularly, all the emotional events surrounding Achille's contact with Ulrich over the last few years.

The sum total of their spiritual discussions can be summarised by quoting from chapter nineteen of St. Mathew's Gospel, verses three to twelve:

Some Pharisees approached Jesus and to test him they said, 'Is it against the Law for a man to divorce his wife on any pretext whatever?' He answered, 'Have you not read that the creator from the beginning made them male and female and that he said: This is why a man must leave father and mother and cling to his wife and the two become one body? They are no longer two, therefore but one body. So then, what God united, man must not divide.'

They said to him, 'Then why did Moses command that a writ of dismissal should be given in cases of divorce?' 'It was because you were so unteachable' he said 'that Moses allowed you to divorce your wives but it was not like this from the beginning. Now I say this to you: the man who divorces his wife - I am not speaking of fornication - and marries another, is guilty of adultery.'

The disciples said to him, 'If that is how things are between husband and wife, it is not advisable to marry.' But he replied, 'It is not everyone who can accept what I have said but only to those to whom it is granted. There are eunuchs born that way from their mother's womb, there are eunuchs made so by men and there are eunuchs who have made themselves that way for the sake of the kingdom of heaven. Let anyone accept this who can.'

****

Achille thought long and hard about their discussion over the next few months, particularly the last part of the penultimate sentence - *there are eunuchs who have made themselves that way for the sake of the kingdom of heaven.*

The irony of the situation was not lost on Achille. He felt that God was calling for self-imposed celibacy which he'd rejected as a young man, the very reason he was not a priest. His spiritual life seemed finally to have come full circle after some thirty-five years in the wilderness. He had been afraid to become a priest for fear of breaking a vow of celibacy, yet he had broken his marriage vow - until death us do part. Could he really become celibate at the age of fifty-one? Having re-married, he had to consider Miriam's needs as well? It seemed like catch twenty-two?

The turmoil in his mind and soul was now a constant backdrop to his everyday life; there was an undeniable inner force that drove him towards resolving his spiritual dilemma. He became ever more conscious of two biblical passages, ones he'd no doubt heard as a young man. They must have been lurking in the back of his mind for years, thrust there ever since he'd lapsed, afraid to face the reality of his ever-more moribund spiritual state.

The first spoke of the past: -

What does it profit a man if he gains the whole world but suffers the loss of his soul?

The second spoke of the future: -

You must be made new in mind and spirit and put on a new nature.

Easter was approaching when he finally decided to go to confession. He'd become morally forced by his conscience to this decision. Confession is forever secret in this world; we shall never know what passed between them. A priest swears never to reveal what's said, on pain of death.

Achille was truly penitent over the mess he'd made of his spiritual life; as a consequence he was left to resolve the problem his decision created, the one between him and Miriam. He knew he had a strong and loving marriage. He felt it could stand the strain of his desire to become a celibate practising Catholic once more. He was about to find out?

Miriam was only vaguely aware of his early years. He spoke to her at length, told her about his original vocation and the way in which his conscience had been re-ignited by all the events surrounding Ulrich. He now felt he wanted to be a Catholic by conviction, not by an accident of birth and upbringing. He wanted to put matters right between himself and God. He knew he was asking a great deal of her.

Miriam became very upset. She also was a divorcee. She felt cheated. She had not married a Catholic and she started crying. Was he asking her for a divorce?

Achille said "No way!" Whilst he'd made his promise to her in a Registry Office and not a church, he'd made it and meant it absolutely. He loved her dearly. Having broken his vows once, he had no intention of breaking such a promise for a second time. He had no desire to do such a thing. What he was really asking her was, did she love him enough for them to be able to live as brother and sister in a loving but celibate relationship?

The strain on their relationship showed up in the next few weeks, long silences, cool body language and monosyllabic conversation. Both Amber and Olivia had left home and were married by this time, Miriam moved into one of the other bedrooms, adding to the strained relationship which now ran into a second month. Achille half-feared but accepted the idea that Miriam might have an affaire or move out altogether if she found someone else.

Their love for each other, like all good marriages, was not based solely on sex but on love, depth of character, a shared understanding of their work, their home life, their family life and the promise of a shared existence and the joy of grandchildren to come. It had become a honed and rounded way of life, built over many years of a close loving relationship, where even absence made the heart grow fonder ... It survived!

Strange as it seemed to Achille, his love for Miriam increased, stemming from her understanding of his spiritual need. As a practicing Catholic he was now at peace. This showed in his unspoken but overt gratitude to Miriam.

Miriam came to recognise the difference in him. Where once his life seemed frenetic, travelling hither and thither, filling his time with one activity after another, he now devoted more time to her and the family. He no longer wanted the world, just her, his family and his faith. He was more contented.

****

Sometime after this change came about, his sister Emma told him that one afternoon, some years ago, when she visited their mother, she found her sitting in her armchair saying the Rosary. Mother had remarked, as she put the Rosary aside, "I say it most days, praying that Achille will one day come back to the Church.

There was a surprising sequel to this reconciliation. One morning at breakfast, some two years later, quite out of the blue, Miriam said, "You should be pleased."

"Why's that?" Asked Achille.

"I've decided I'd like to become a Catholic."

****

Twenty-two

Dear Pascal,

For some little time I have been subscribing to the *'Tablet'*, a Catholic weekly magazine. I don't know if there is a French equivalent? I'll enclose a copy for you to look at.

When you invited me to stay for dinner, the first time we met, you may remember we talked about each of our discussions with Ulrich. I mentioned that I'd asked him if he thought the bible was true? His reply was yes, with some understandable reservations. Well in last week's *'Tablet'* there was an interesting article on the astronomy associated with the coming of the Magi.

It discussed a new computer programme that was able to backtrack the movement of stars and planets, etc. I was impressed by the outcome of a long 'backwardation' of 'heavenly movements that had been completed recently.

I thought you would be interested as it gives a very clear tick on the side of biblical truth. I've built the findings, given in the article, into the story of the Epiphany, taken from chapter two of St. Matthew's gospel; I hope you like it? I certainly enjoyed your detailed expansion of the beginning of the universe and the world, given in Genesis.

Kindest regards

Achille

The Epiphany

Isaiah, when prophesying the birth of Christ, said: - *But on you the light of the Lord will shine; the brightness of his presence will be with you. Nations will be drawn to your light and kings to the dawning of your new day.*

Great caravans of camels will come, from Median and Ephah; they will come from Sheba, bringing gold and incense!

Mankind, in many parts of the world, had become aware of and studied the apparent movement of the stars. In Babylon, these movements were used to time the first calendar c.530 BC. Other people interpreted the movement of stars as signs and portents of worldly events to come.

One such portent was the heliacal rising of a star (that is, when it rises and becomes visible at dawn, just before the full light of sunrise 'drowns it out'). In astrological terms the three wise men believed it heralded the birth of a great king. They observed such an event in the east, in a constellation they associated with Judea. So they set out to take gifts to the king and pay homage.

Jesus was born in the town of Bethlehem in Judea, during the time when Herod was king. Soon afterwards, some men who studied the stars came from the east to Jerusalem and asked, "Where is the baby born to be the king of the Jews? We saw his star when it came up in the east and we have come to worship him." But nobody knew.

As they came into Jerusalem the star disappeared, (the moon was passing in front of it - an occultation, so they went to King Herod, thinking it would be his progeny but, of course, it was not.

When King Herod heard about this, he was very upset and so was everyone else in Jerusalem. He called together all the chief priests and the teachers of the law and asked them, "Where will the Messiah be born?"

"In the town of Bethlehem in Judea," they answered, for this is what the prophet wrote:

Bethlehem in the land of Judah, you are by no means the least of the leading cities of Judah; for from you will come a leader who will guide my people Israel. `

So Herod called the visitors from the east to a secret meeting and ... he sent them to Bethlehem...

The Magi left Herod and approached Bethlehem from the west. The time span of occultation of the star (In fact it was Jupiter, which at that time was thought to be a star) had now passed.

And so they left and on their way they saw the same star they had seen in the east. When they saw it, how happy they were, what joy was theirs! It went ahead of them until it stopped over the place where the child was.

(Now comes the tricky bit about relative motion, a bit like the effect of two trains, side-by-side, moving at slightly different speeds. The Earth is moving faster in its orbit around the sun than Jupiter. It was 'overtaking' Jupiter, thus creating an optical illusion. The alignment of the two planets caused Jupiter to appear to become stationary against the background of stars as the Earth moved that bit faster. The computer backwardation shows that this sequence of events actually took place in 6 BC; Jupiter appeared to stand still in Israel on the 17th of April!)

They went into the house and when they saw the child with his mother Mary, they knelt down and worshipped him. They brought their gifts of gold, frankincense and myrrh and presented them to him.

****

Dear Achille,

I thought you would be interested in the fact that I've found three more references in the bible, to support Max's idea that a soul (*spirit* not *breath* this time) was given to humankind - thus creating mankind:

The most important perhaps is from either the psalms or Judges I think, (sorry but I've lost my note of the reference). *You spoke, they were made. You sent forth your spirit and it formed them.* Two sentences two distinct steps?

From Psalm 104 v. 30. *But when you sent out your spirit, they were created.* By implication it was a second step that created mankind?

Finally from the prophet Ezekiel, 36: 27). *I will put my spirit in you and I will see to it that you follow my laws and keep all the commands I have given you.* A statement that reinforces the fact that God put a spirit in humankind - and that he then gave guidance to mankind - to show the way mankind should live its life?

I think that in creating mankind, God gave humankind the greatest possible gift that he could bestow, a likeness to Himself, with the promise that we can share heaven with Him, who formed us all, if we so choose.

The other reason for writing is because I've come across some potentially good news. It has always troubled me and you perhaps, that if Ulrich was right to separate mankind from humankind, it begs the question, what happened to all the rest of humankind after Adam and Eve were created? We are all said to have descended from them, so what happened to all the corporeal beings?

A recent article appeared in *Nature*. It leads one to the conclusion that Max's idea could in fact be correct. In summary it says, "by using a computer model, researchers at MIT attempted to trace back our ancestry through common DNA markers, using estimated patterns of migration throughout history. They concluded that we are all from a common ancestor who lived in Asia, around 1415 BC.

They go on to say that they found a time when a large fraction of people (mankind?) had developed - while the rest (humankind?) were ancestors of no one alive today; that was around 5353 BC? Dr. Steve Olsen, who led the research, stressed that the dates were only rough estimates at this stage.

It tends to confirm Ulrich's contention but the dates don't make a great deal of sense at the moment. It does raise the prospect that if and when such DNA research becomes more sophisticated and the backtracking programme on computers is more accurate, things could well clarify. It might be that the 5353 BC and 1415 BC dates eventually meld to become 3927 BC and the stock of humankind dies out thereafter?

Finally, I refer you back to the letter you wrote to me in '81. I originally thought Ulrich and Leonard Osrow were a little mad with their idea that the Universe was possibly only eight billion years old but then you sent me the book by Dr. Joao Magueijo, 'Faster than the Speed of Light' on VSL theory.

A recent article I've read adds weight to the idea that the speed of light can change. It was a report from the American Association for the Advancement of Science. A team at the Rowland Institute, in Cambridge Massachusetts, has succeeded in slowing down the speed of light. I don't pretend to understand the details but I thought you'd be interested.

In summary it said that Professor Lene Hau's team had shown that the speed of light could be slowed to a 'crawl'. In the experiment, they had reduced the temperature of sodium atoms, chilled them down to one-millionth of a degree above absolute zero. At this point the atoms merged to form, what is called, a Bose-Einstein condensate, whatever that is? Once the condensate was created, a 'coupling' laser, tuned to resonate with the trapped mass of atoms was beamed into the trap-chamber so that the atoms and photons of light become 'entangled'. A pulsed laser probe was then shot into the 'laser-dressed' condensate from a different laser - it was the latter light that was slowed to a "crawl" from its normal 186,000 miles per second.

Here, for the first time, is an experiment that proves that the speed of light can change, or be made to change! Albeit slower rather than faster.

Regards
Pascal

****

PartThree

1986 - 2005

Twenty-three

In the eight years since the Post War Finance Committee's decision to search Achille's house and/or kidnap him, a great deal had changed. All six of the original members had either died or decided to retire, as had Otto Altmann and Herman Fritz the somewhat younger replacement chairman and secretary.

To eliminate previous security problems, the latter two had recruited new, like-minded Germans, as a replacement cadre in Europe. Its remit was to obtain as much as possible of the £43 million being released from the 'hidden' Swiss funds. It took three years for the new unit to recover £3.75 million, at which point the remainder of the 'old guard' resigned.

The Nazis had successfully gone to ground after the war and had been financed by committee controlled funds. They'd mainly set up businesses but not exclusively across South America; had married or re-married and had families. There were significant residual funds due to a very well controlled investment portfolio by the old Finance Committee.

The new generation had been brought up with a hatred of Jews and a strong dislike of the English and Americans. Four sons formed a new committee to control these funds. All the families were well established now so these four wanted to use the funds at their disposal to attack the Jews and exact vengeance on the two allies for the defeat of the Fatherland. They felt very strongly that the monies should be used to act against the interests of all three nations. Led by Klaus Mecklenbeck, they recognised that the money gave them a unique opportunity and they had the stomach for the 'fight'.

The new European cadre had recruited personnel in the USA, the UK and within the Middle Eastern countries opposed to Israel. The three territories were where the majority of Jewish holocaust survivors had found sanctuary. The new people had built contacts within the banks, the police, the civil service and among some criminal elements. The new committee had arms-length control of this well-established network via generous funding.

The four had met in 1986, debated and agreed on the new strategy, "To undermine the power and international reputation of the two allies and to work for the destruction of Israel." This had been the prime purpose behind setting up the teams.

Their funds would be used to enter and develop the lucrative drug trade that would eat away at the heart of these three nations. More importantly, the significant additional sums generated could then be used to fund the development of a fifth column within the countries.

They invested in the drugs trade in the USA initially, their ruthless approach ultimately penetrating the top management levels until they exercised a controlling interest in at least two key groups. The UK followed.

As their new income became assured, they backed anti-Israeli factions in Syria and Lebanon as well as Palestinian groups living amongst the Jews. They had been gratified by the emergence of radical Islamic groups which were not of their making, who also wanted to fight the Jews and other infidels. They did all they could to encourage them.

****

Twenty-four

Achille's health had deteriorated to some degree and Miriam had persuaded him that he could well afford to retire. She also retired in 1997 and they went on a month's holiday to the Far East.

They flew from London to Tokyo on the new non-stop service via northern Russia. They stayed at the *Okura* hotel near the American embassy where President Regan had stayed when he visited Japan. They were charmed by the novel wake-up call, a recording of the dawn chorus. With four restaurants to choose from and a parade of shops, they were in the lap of luxury.

They took a trip on the Bullet Train to Osaka; they also went on an organised trip, to Kyoto to visit some of the key historical sites of Japanese culture. They went on a day trip into the mountains to experience the hot spring baths, a ritual aspect of Japanese life. They went to a Kabuki theatre, a Pachinko parlour and something that originated in Japan, a Karaoke bar. They were very impressed with the cleanliness, politeness self-discipline and general conduct of the society. It made a wonderful first week to their holiday.

From there they flew down to Bangkok. Achille in particular wanted to visit his somewhat estranged son Samuel who had moved there many years before, initially working in the off-shore oil industry. He had married a Thai girl, Sumai, whom Achille and Miriam had never met. Samuel had booked them into the *Emerald* hotel, near to where he and his wife lived.

The hotel was excellent, a high-class business hotel off the tourist trail.

It had two restaurants and a bar by a swimming pool on the roof, ideal for sun bathing, cooling in the pool and generally relaxing. A nice touch was a fresh orchid on each of their pillows every night. Samuel had organised his holiday from the university where he now taught English to coincide with his Dad's and Miriam's visit. They went out as a foursome to a variety of Thai restaurants most evenings, enjoying the food, catching up on their lives in conversation and enjoying the floor shows which seemed to concentrate on various aspect of traditional Thai dancing.

They visited the old capital of Ayutthaya by train, quite an experience in itself, saw the very old ruins and visited the summer residence and grounds of the King, on the outskirts of that city. On another occasion they went on an organised day trip to Kanchanaburri to see the bridge over the river Khwae, the preserved prisoner of war camps, the allied cemeteries and took a boat trip on the river as well as a train ride on a section of the infamous Burma railway.

They went to see the very famous royal palace in Bangkok with all its gold leaf and the Emerald Buddha. Miriam's abiding memory was of a high-speed trip in a long-tailed boat on the klongs of Bangkok, which included a visit to the floating market. On another day they all took a bus for the seventy miles down to Pattaya to visit an orphanage, a charity with which Achille had become involved. The ladies thought it might be too upsetting to see the deaf, blind and disabled children, so only Achille and Samuel visited whilst Sumai and Miriam got to know one another on a tour of the shops. In spite of Sumai's halting English, a strong rapport developed.

Pattaya is a beautiful seaside resort with a great beach that grew from a fishing village into what was almost a city, as a place for 'Rest and Relaxation' by the American forces, during the Vietnamese War.

After a wonderful two weeks in Thailand, getting to know his son again, they flew further down the Asian peninsula to Singapore, where they stayed at the *Royal Orchid* hotel. They were impressed with the floral displays almost everywhere they went. It was a quiet time of rest and relaxation after the rather hectic schedule of sightseeing the previous three weeks.

They noticed in particular the large Chinese element in the population and the huge monsoon drainage works on the island. They only took one trip, a coach outing across the Johor Strait into Malaysia. It rained a lot of the day causing the coach to slide off the road on a bend taken a bit too fast, into a shallow ditch. All the passengers got out and got wet, when a passing lorry driver agreed to pull it back onto the road. They saw pineapple plantations and visited a seaside village built on stilts out over the water at a place called Kukup on the southwest coast. Later in the afternoon the weather improved, so they had a more relaxing return to Singapore.

They were pleased to get home, flying Singapore - London, at the end of a very memorable four weeks.

****

Achille and Miriam got involved with church matters in their retirement, enjoyed spending time working and relaxing in the garden, going to the cinema, reading and listening to music.

It was quite a few years since Achille had met Pascal. A few months into their retirement, he persuaded them to come down to Lyon for a long weekend. Pascal met them at Satolas and made them very welcome. Miriam thought Lyon was really lovely. They took full advantage of the fine local cuisine in some wonderful restaurants.

One of Achille's activities that blossomed in retirement, more so after their visit to Lyon, was corresponding with Pascal. They seemed somehow to feed off each other, especially when it came to matters relating to Ulrich and what he'd had to say.

Dear Pascal,

When we got back from our very enjoyable Easter weekend with you, I came across an article on quantum computers that will be a quantum leap in computer technology (please excuse the pun).

It gave rise to a train of thought. You know how something can sometimes trigger an all-embracing instant mental picture, so it was with this.

It takes longer to explain than the thought itself. It went something like this. The telephone - the radio - the teleprinter - television - electronic computers - global communications - the Internet - computer voice recognition - voice synthesis - then it jelled into a 'picture' of future events. I decided to give my imagination free rein for once.

People rarely listen to speeches, normally just to broadcasts of highlights on news programmes. But now I know how it might change - the novelty of a new instant-translation capability.

Our very great thanks for a lovely weekend and our kindest regards.

Achille

The Final Advance in World Communications ?

The article explained that the origin of quantum computers goes back to the 1970s. Theorists, Feymann and Deutsch among others, thought-through the theoretical concept of shrinking microelectronics down to the atomic level. This would bring future computers into the realm of quantum mechanics using photons of light, maybe individual electrons or even the spinning nuclei of atoms, to process data. Atomic nuclei can be seen to be 'on' and 'off', or 'plus' and 'minus', at the same time, unlike conventional computers. They can be seen from at least two directions simultaneously. This they called a qubit.

It would appear that for twenty years many scientists have lived with this dream. Such a computer would be smaller, have vastly greater capacity and by doing two things at once, would be at lest twice as fast, probably faster.

In 1994 Peter Shor described an algorithm to find the factors of a number. An academic exercise really but current computers could take weeks, months, or even years factoring large numbers - yet once done, it is simple to verify by multiplication. Apparently many organisations now use this approach as a firewall to protect confidential information held in computers.

Shor's algorithm set many scientists thinking once more about their dream - a quantum computer. Isaac Chuang was able to show that quantum computing was theoretically possible. He started experimenting, using a beaker of fluid to show that the spin of a single atomic nucleus could be 'read' with magnetic resonance, as developed and used in medical MRI scanners. He set out to adapt and apply this technology to a suitable fluid.

Mr. Chuang's colleagues at IBM designed and made a new molecule for this purpose. It consisted of five atoms of fluorine and two of carbon - seven nuclei that would allow factorisation problems to be addressed. Pulses of a radio frequency were used to programme a phial of this liquid, the movements of which were then detected by magnetic resonance. The challenge was to have sufficient control of the process for the purpose of computation. This was crudely achieved for the fist time at the end of 2000. The experimental set-up found the factors of fifteen - three and five.

Recently Mr, Chuang and his colleagues were able to demonstrate this infant quantum computer to the scientific press. Nabil Amer of IBM said at the demonstration, "This result reinforces the growing realisation that quantum computers may some day be able to solve problems that are so complex that even the most powerful (electronic) super-computers, working for millions of years, could not calculate the answers".

Eventually from this small beginning there will come the ultimate in computers.

So, based on this article, I've let my imagination take over and tried to emulate what Max might have thought, prompted by a sentence in the Old Testament: -

The city was called Babylon, because there the Lord mixed up the language of all the people.

With the advent of quantum computers, I can readily foresee them having the capacity and speed to cope with simultaneous language translation. This could be a major step in international understanding, eliminating bias and spin in the reporting of what they think is meant by what is said.

Voice recognition exists but choosing the equivalent word in a foreign language will require very speedy analysis of the context. One would not want to confuse 'pawn' for 'porn, or 'not' with 'knot', or 'caught' with 'court', or 'to' with 'two' for example. So it would need to analyse the meaning of the word, from its context, before it chose an equivalent.

This advance in communications will come from the existence of new quantum computers, driven initially by a worldwide demand from the broadcasting media. It will happen when a bright young programmer designs a new bi-lingual programme, incorporating the analytical process. He or she will probably call it *Babylon I* for obvious reasons. It will enable the quantum computer to produce simultaneous language translation for the very first time, in conjunction with voice recognition and synthesis. In subsequent years, bi-lingual databases for over one hundred and fifty different languages will eventually become available for use with this programme by most nations on earth.

This 'instant' translation capability, combined with the much-improved quality of electronic voice recognition and voice generation, will take the quantum computer to unprecedented levels of performance. Later, further sophistication in, say a *Babylon II* programme, will provide the ability to generate inflection, emphasis, timbre and perhaps even regional accents?

As quantum computers spread throughout the broadcasting world, a network of bi-lateral and multi-lateral agreements will be built up. Ultimately any broadcast, in any language, anywhere, will be able to be heard in the local language of another country, at virtually the same instant, if placed on the TV or radio network.

The ever-improving voice recognition and voice synthesis translation capability will then be added to the international telephone system. Due to the multi-ethnic mix of society, it might also be offered on domestic telephone networks eventually.

In a separate strand of programming, typed text recognition or, if you will, computer reading, will be somewhat easier to accomplish. There could then be a multi-lingual translation capability from print or typescript that could be used to translate books, articles and letters. It could also be made available to Internet users. This will complete an unprecedented worldwide communication capability where language is no longer a barrier to communication and understanding.

It brings to mind chapter two in the Acts of the Apostles, verses five to eleven, albeit some two thousand years later. Clearly we will need a lot of sophisticated equipment to even begin to emulate what God did with people's minds on this occasion.

There were Jews living in Jerusalem, religious men who had come from every country in the world. When they heard this noise, a large crowd gathered. They were all excited, because each of them heard the believers speaking in his own language. In amazement and wonder they exclaimed,

"These people who are talking like this are Galileans! How is it, then, that all of us hear them speaking in our own languages? We are from Parthia, Media and Elam; from Mesopotamia, Judaea and Cappadocia; from Pontus and Asia, from Phrygia and Pamphylia, from Egypt and the regions of Libya near Cyrene. Some of us are from Rome, both Jews and gentiles converted to Judaism and some of us are from Crete and Arabia - Yet all of us hear them speaking in our own languages about the great things God has done!"

****

Twenty-five

In the year 2002, the fifty-sixth meeting of the Post War Finance Committee was being held, it was being held as if the four had met for a game of cards in Mecklenbeck's home.

A great deal had occurred to feed their antagonism against America, Britain and Israel. The USA's backing of Israel in the Arab-Israeli wars, its war in Afghanistan, then the war with Iraq over Kuwait - all fuelled their hatred.

There were compensations. The lucrative drug trade in America and the UK had developed beyond their expectations. The money was rolling in and their enemies societies were being undermined, morally, physically and to some degree, economically.

More importantly, Al Queda had come on the scene, a strong Moslem organisation showing the way. They organised the most brilliant act of terrorism so far, the destruction of the twin towers trade centre in New York.

The probable invasion of Iraq, by the USA and Britain, underlined the committee's desire to cause as much grief for them as possible. It was decisive action they now craved.

They agreed to fund two additional projects:

- To strengthen their personnel and thus their contacts in Syria and Iran with a view to fostering an insurgency programme of disruption in Iraq.

It was clear that the Allies would prevail in Iraq, through unequalled military might. But they foresaw that where Saddam Hussein had held the country together by brute force as had Tito in Yugoslavia before him, post war Iraq, like Yugoslavia, could easily be made to become a hotbed of factional infighting between Kurds, Sunni and Shiite Moslems. This could hopefully lead to another humiliating Vietnam-like scenario.

- To make it known to the PLO, Hamas, Hezbollah, Al Queda and Iran, that the cost of obtaining an atomic bomb for a strike against Israel, would be met by them. In spite of all the efforts of the last fifty-six years, none of Israel's enemies had succeeded in reducing that country to its knees, largely due to massive American support. Now was the time to take a decisive step, end the problem of the Jews once and for all.

The Russian situation led them to believe that obtaining an atomic bomb, via the 'black market', was a distinct possibility.

Twenty-six

The last remnants of the cold front had passed. The rain had ceased whilst they were in church. Now a watery sun was breaking through as they all stood on the damp muddy grass around the open grave. Tears ran down Miriam and Olivia's cheeks, accompanied by shuddering sobs, as wife and daughter watched Achille's coffin being slowly lowered into the wet ground. As he grew older and his heart grew weaker the inevitability of death did nothing to lessen their grief at his very sudden passing. The three of them had been close.

Years ago he'd told Olivia how he'd fondled her on his shoulder when she was less than an hour old - his own daughter. How he knew intuitively in that moment that she was special to him. She realised that there had always been that something between them, a bond that reached maturity when he and Miriam had taken her into their new home, away from her troublesome stepfather.

Miriam was equally distraught. They'd had a wonderful marriage which had lasted almost forty years. Amber was supporting her. Achille had been a good dad to her and she would miss him greatly. All three of them were grateful to have become Catholics. They truly believed in the after-life which was a great comfort.

Samuel and Sumai, along with other close family, lingered round the open grave, comforting one another, putting off the moment of departure, the final goodbye. Olivia, Miriam and Amber said a silent prayer of thanks for his very special relationship and the added spiritual insight he'd finally brought into their lives after his own journey of faith with Ulrich.

Miriam had phoned Olivia to gently tell her of her father's sudden passing from a heart attack. She'd surprised and pleased her when she'd gone on to ask her if she would organise the funeral and choose the readings and hymns for the Requiem Mass.

Miriam had also 'phoned Samuel in Thailand. They'd become closer since Achille's retirement holiday. It transpired that he'd been promising Sumai a visit to England, now was the time he kept that promise.

Olivia thought back over the last few years after her father had retired. How she'd enjoyed listening to the stories of a unique hermit - Ulrich Hoffman, alias Max Seiber. How the story had made her, Amber and Miriam follow him into the Catholic Church.

She'd woken this morning, dreading the day, a feeling made worse by heavy rain from a leaden sky. Their parish church, dating from the late 1880s, had a sombre Victorian air as they entered behind the pallbearers. Olivia was pleasantly surprised however at the number of parishioners, family, friends and acquaintances that seemed to fill the church.

Then came Father John's opening words, "We are here to celebrate the life of Achille Aarden," which had brought more tears to her eyes. As the Mass progressed, she was comforted and pleased by the words of the readings and hymns she'd chosen.

She was particularly appreciative of the eulogy given by Father Alan Walton. They'd renewed their old friendship. As his spiritual advisor Alan came to know Achille even better. He made her father's life seem very special indeed. She felt really proud to be his daughter.

The gathering after the funeral offered some distraction. Olivia talked to her uncles, aunts and cousins that she'd not seen for some years, spent time with Samuel and Sumai who were staying with Miriam, and with Father Alan. She also chatted with friends of the family, including one or two of her father's closest friends from his work which gave her new insights to his business life.

Miriam knew how close Olivia had become to her father since he'd retired. She asked Olivia if she'd mind helping her with her father's effects. Olivia was pleased to help sort out her father's things rather than sit around at home and mope once Casper had to go on his next trip.

As she and Miriam went through the things in his study, Miriam told her what her father had said, "Olivia's to have first choice from my books," so Olivia spent some time looking through them. Thinking of Miriam, she decided to take only four.

"What have you chosen?"

"Well, you remember he told us a lot of stories about the Swiss hermit he met during his business travels. I've picked books to remind me of those stories. A book called *'Charles Kingsley and his Ideas'*, by Kingsley's wife - A Penguin *'Dictionary of the Third Reich'*, a detailed Swiss atlas and an old book that includes Switzerland - *'Boswell on the Grand Tour'*. They'll bring back nice memories and it will be interesting to read about what Switzerland was like a hundred and fifty years ago."

Miriam said, "You told us that you'd started to write a book, to fill the time when Casper and the boys are away. I know from what you've said, it's about your father, I thought you might like to borrow these. This picture of the *'Eremitage'* was hanging on the wall in our bedroom. You probably remember his mother gave it to him and this loose-leaf folder. I've read it these last few days and I'm sure you will find it interesting, it's the one Ulrich bequeathed to him. It now has lots of his correspondence with Pascal, added to it, which could perhaps, influence your story. The picture's got an envelope stuck on the back, containing some photos."

"That's really thoughtful of you Miriam," she said, bursting into tears. Her emotions were still very close to the surface. They hugged each other until their sobs and tears subsided.

The following day Olivia couldn't help thinking about how much she'd miss her father, the special place he'd held in her heart. The odd tear trickled down her cheek as she looked at the photos behind the picture. There was the one she remembered of her father crouching at the Iona-style cross, water fountain when he was four. Then two she hadn't seen that must have been taken when he took Miriam to Switzerland. One of Miriam with the hermitage in the background and one of her father crouching at the water fountain, same pose but in his late 50s.

There was also a tourist leaflet, one her father must have picked up. It gave a potted history of the Verena gorge.

She began to read the contents of the folder, Ulrich's original code sheets with her father's solutions, then the many pages of letters to and from Pascal. She was surprised at how much it contained. As she progressed, it took her mind back to the story she'd been told about Ulrich's life as a cryptographer and then as an eremite. Finally she came to the last three pages and they surprised her, the last one in particular.

The first of these, she saw, was cut from the *'Spectator'* magazine. Highlighted was a quotation by Paul Johnson.

"The modern world is Freud, Hitler and Stalin. It is Auschwitz and the gulag; it is Aids and anorexia, crack and speed, Hiroshima and the killing fields, San Francisco bathhouses and Bangkok brothels. At its miserable best it is down market tabloids, Disneyland and channel four soft porn. At its worst it is human degradation so complete and cruelty so heartless as to leave Satan and his pandemonium gasping with pride at their creation. For it is they who brought the modern world into this depraved existence."

Achille had written in the margin - 'As I get older these words strike me ever more forcibly. They express my feelings far better than I ever could. The decline in people's standards - how it questions the modern way of life and by implication, it conveys the eschewing of religious belief.

The second page was from the *'Tablet'*. Highlighted was a quote by John Wilkins:

"One must warn the gullible multitude about the abysses of grief to which the modern world inexorably leads."

Again he'd made a note in the margin - When I saw it, I thought it would make a very fitting end to this folder but it also led me to an idea about Olivia's writing - *'warning the gullible multitude etc'*.

The third page brought floods of tears; it was a hand written note, specifically addressed to her. It must have been written only weeks before he died.

Dear Olivia,

When you read this I will have died. I know you are writing a romance, loosely based on my earlier, rather shameful life. Might I suggest that you re-think the plot to incorporate my return to the church?

Mindful of the quote on the previous page, motivated by it in fact, I ask you to write it in such a way that it becomes a spark to the spirit, one that lights a fire, the gift of faith within the readers' soul.

Miriam, you and Amber followed me into the church. There are many more out there who need to understand what is really at stake as they live their lives!

All the best with your endeavours my love, I know you'll do it well.

Eternal love.

Dad

****

Part Four

_2007 – 3913_

Twenty-seven

Olivia had thought long and hard in re-planning her book. It was a lengthy debate within her mind, whether these last letters and notes, written by her father, should come before or after his funeral?

On balance she decided they should come after, for three reasons. First, they seemed to make a fitting end to the book. Second was the fact that they dealt with the end of the world and they somehow counterbalanced Pascal's expansion of the book of Genesis. And third was the fact that she herself had only read them after his death.

****

Dear Pascal,

I enjoyed writing that piece on quantum computers; I then had a desire to follow that figment of my imagination with another. I decided to do something more ambitious concerning the last one thousand nine hundred years, from now to the end of time. You wrote that nice piece on how the world began, here's my piece on events that might occur.

Emulating Ulrich, I decided to use biblical words that prompt a train of thought. Jesus himself draws our attention to their importance –

"Listen!" Says Jesus, "I am coming soon! Happy are those who obey the prophetic words in this book!"

(Rev. 22: 7)

What I found and what Ulrich had to say, has, to a very large extent, dictated the scenario of the events I outline.

The second biblical quote sets the temporal scene:

199

There is going to be a time of great distress,
Unparalleled since nations first came into existence.
(Dan. 12; 1)

HG Wells gave a succinct summary of our problem.

"Human history becomes more and more a race between education and catastrophe. The education needed is the sharing of wisdom, our knowledge of the natural world has raced far ahead of our wisdom to use it."

I hope you find it makes interesting reading and that it proves to be a fruitful source of reflection.

My kindest regards

Achille

World history was once classified by the key material of the time. The Stone Age, the Bronze Age and the Iron Age for example. But now all materials meld into one idea - the Materialist Age.

Materialism is also indicative of a change of emphasis, not materials *per se* but their consumption. Starting with the Industrial Revolution, it will probably end with the emergence of sustainable materials re-cycling economy - The Post Materialist Age.

By 1900 the emergent industries used some twenty of the eighty-two elements, then known to mankind. By 1955, mankind was using all 92 of the naturally occurring elements and by the year 2000, two additional man-made elements as well.

There was an eighty-three fold increase in iron and steel production from 1900 to 1913 and a further six fold increase by 1995. There was a twenty-two-fold increase in the demand for copper over the same period. Aluminium production saw the biggest growth - a three thousand-fold increase in the hundred years of the 20th century.

From 1963 to 1995 the production of materials entering the

global economy, doubled from five billion to ten billion tons. Mankind had developed a mindset of materialism, becoming a profligate, disposable society of pure consumerism. Rates of growth in consumption will go beyond sustainability as India, China and others add to the already heavy demand.

Some product prices have become so low it is cheaper to throw products away and buy new ones, rather than have them repaired.

"Foolish people! How long do you want to be foolish? How long will you enjoy pouring scorn on knowledge? Will you never learn? (Prov: 1. 22 - 27)

Mankind had been given a warning as early as 1958 with the "Cod War". The next renewable resource shortage was wood in the 1990s. The consumption of paper caused the felling of suitable trees to exceed the supply. In consequence the economics of collecting paper started to become viable creating the birth of a new growth industry - recycling.

"I appeal to you mankind; I call to everyone on earth. Are you immature? Learn to be mature. Are you foolish? Learn to have sense." (Prov: 8. 4 - 5)

The reality of some real shortages will probably start to bite from around 2050. It is almost as if God had timed it to coincide with the fossil fuel shortage and the peak of climate change problems; everything seeming to be going wrong at once.

...when it comes on you like a storm, bringing fierce winds of trouble and you are in pain and misery. (Prov: 1. 27)

****

The finite amount of fossil fuel in the world's deposits, one could say, is both the cause of the greenhouse effect and its potential solution. Because God only gave us this amount, when we run out, it will stop us from ruining our planet's environment completely. We will have learned enough technology; it now presents mankind with the problem of having to work out an alternative energy solution.

There has already been a sixteen-fold increase in the cost of energy over the last fifty years. As early as 2015 - 20, the cost of energy could create civil unrest, initiating a growing sense of doom. A downward spiral in the world's economic activity will be the consequence of excessive fuel price.

The seeds of the change can be traced in the past when Jules Verne had Captain Nemo say water was the fuel of the future. Then next Haldane's lecture in 1923, in which he suggested that electricity could be generated from wind to produce hydrogen via the electrolysis of water, then liquefied, stored and distributed as a fuel. The final seed came in the 1930s when Hastings and Campbell showed that an internal combustion engine could be run on hydrogen.

Lessing wrote in 1961, "Hydrogen is the Master Fuel of a New Age".

God made a home in the sky for the sun; it comes out in the morning like a happy bridegroom, like an athlete eager to run a race. It starts out at one end of the sky and goes across to the other. Nothing can hide from its heat. (Ps: 19. 4 - 6)

Saudi-Arabia will set up a post-oil action committee, the outcome of which will be to invest heavily in an experimental Solar - Hydrogen production scheme, via the electrolysis of water. From this small step will emerge the hydrogen fuelled economy of the future.

A man called Hildebrandt had proposed a mirror concentrator method for the conversion of water into hydrogen by the use of solar energy. The Rub al Khali desert offers up to 150,000 square miles of the world's highest insolation area. The Saudis are rich enough to take such a gamble; the first step towards a hydrogen fuelled economy.

By 2021 the escalating price of oil and gas, combined with the ongoing efficiency gains of solar energy produced hydrogen, will ensure a competitive edge for the "new" fuel.

The USA, not to be outdone, will make ambitious plans with three different projects. A Californian Solarstation will follow the Saudi Arabian high insolation route. An Aerostation will use a vast array of wind generators on the Pacific Coast. A small experimental Seastation off the coast of Florida will use the ocean thermal gradient of the Gulf Stream.

Lawaczeck suggested in the 1930s that it would be cheaper to transmit energy in pipes. Lindstrom did some comparison studies which confirmed that the use of gas pipelines for distribution would cost only 20% of that for electric wires! So in the second half of the twenty-first century, new hydrogen gas pipelines will effectively span the world.

****

By 2025 the pre-industrial revolution level of carbon dioxide in the atmosphere will have doubled. By this date it will be increasing at the rate of 4% per annum. At this level of growth it will double every eighteen years but India and China's economic expansion will make it accelerate ever faster.

Torrents of rain will pour down from the sky   (Is: 24.18)

Recent world history reveals that where there were six major flood disasters in the 1950s, there were seven in the 1960s, eight in the 1970s, eighteen in the 1980s and twenty-six in the 1990s. It is forecast that there will be some thirty-eight in this, the first decade of the 2000s, probably about fifty-seven in the 2010s, after which they will become the norm.

One hundred million people live within three feet of mean sea level; by 2075 the oceans will have risen this amount, with frightening consequences. Richer countries will spend enormous sums on sea defences.

Ocean currents will slowly change their flow patterns, causing some dramatic effects. Great areas of the United States of America, Canada, Europe and the grain growing regions of Russia will all suffer a random decline in average rainfall during the summer growing season and bouts of short, unacceptably intense rain that will wash-off fertile soil at others. This, along with the higher temperature, will become a recipe for disaster.

I sent scorching wind to dry up your crops. (Am: 4.8)

The world's media will literally bring into homes, in dramatic fashion, the growing scale of the world's problems. As these events unfold, minds will turn ever more strenuously towards the question of what alternatives face mankind.

Listen, Wisdom is calling out in the streets and market places. (Prov: 1. 20)

Mankind will be forced to begin the very uncomfortable process of coming to terms with a spiralling decline in its standard of living. Mankind will have to re-learn hunger, cold and privation but most importantly, the husbandry of what little resources it has left.

To have knowledge, you must first have reverence for the Lord. Stupid people have no respect for wisdom and refuse to learn. (Prov: 1.7)

****

Twenty-eight

The group of four, led by Klaus Mecklenbeck, now had controlling interests in their various, well established businesses in Argentina. As their financial 'empire' spread and Argentina moved left politically, they were spending more time abroad, particularly in America. Also, as they got older, they had begun to take one or two weeks holiday from time to time.

On this occasion they had chosen a log cabin in the Wyoming/Montana border area, in the foothills of the Rockies near Yellowstone Park. They were discussing the extent to which their earlier objectives were being met.

They agreed that American influence was now in decline across the world. They felt the turning point had come during Bush's second term. Iraq had gone the way they planned and hoped, just like Yugoslavia – another Vietnam for the Americans. The American nation had voted against Bush in the 2006 elections.

The nation had now lost its desire to be the world's 'police force,' it had proved too costly in money and prestige. They couldn't become isolationist because of their dependence on international fuel supplies.

Herman Fritz came up with a new suggestion, "I'd like to strike another 9/11 type blow to hasten their decline but this time, much bigger. When that Indian Ocean tsunami devastated the coast of Indonesia in particular, I remember reading about the possibility of an Atlantic tsunami that might be caused if half a mountain, on La Palma, fell into the ocean. I think we should organize a bomb, powerful enough to make it happen, a second atomic bomb if needed.

"The tsunami would cross the Atlantic in six to eight hours and devastate the East Coast of America, from Portland in the north, right down to Miami in the south. Some fourteen major cities and at least two others severely damaged. It will also destroy much along the south coast of England and devastate Bermuda in passing."

Klaus Mecklenbeck thought it a great idea. He suggested it be added to the agenda of their next meeting with their Middle East partners. He added, "As we have established our source for the atomic bomb, we could make it two. Our partners are working on the logistics of getting the parts into Israel and presumably a similar plan can be adopted for La Palma?"

Continuing their review, they turned to England. They felt it had been in slow decline ever since the war but the ten year Blair government accelerated the rate of decline. They made a major foreign policy blunder when they 'got into bed' with America over Iraq.

They failed to follow a basic management principle. If one decides on something, words alone don't make it happen, one has to set the organisation in place to make it happen, in this they signally failed.

They became hooked on the right of the individual to do what he or she liked, on the grounds it was their human right. They promoted a multi-ethnic society instead of integration and it all got away from them. Trying to hold it all together and fight our terrorist cells is turning it into a police state where a level or anarchy now reigns.

Their moral fibre's gone. Their education system has been ruined, their health service is a shambles, their manufacturing industry has suffered a major decline, their transport infrastructure is falling apart and the armed forces are in terminal decline. In fact it was only the advent of North Sea oil and gas that delayed the inevitable and that is now coming to an end. They can no longer afford to be a power in the world, only a bit part player.

Turning to Israel, they agreed that they are becoming ever more isolated as American influence weakens. Their enemies surround them. The atom bomb strike our parents undertook to fund, is now only a matter of time, we will soon finish them off and good riddance.

****

The following day the ground shook beneath them. They rushed to the door of the cabin as a sound like thunder assailed their ears. Three escaped what they thought was an earthquake but Manfred Gasser became trapped as he lost his balance on the heaving floor, fell and his legs were crushed by one of the falling logs. He died a slow agonizing death.

Two managed to get to their cars but a boulder from the falling rocks blasted into the air by the volcanic eruption felled Klaus Mecklenbeck as he ran. Stunned, he lay bemused and in agony with a crushed shoulder, then a crushed pelvis, he was stoned to death.

The car driven by Herman Fritz was stopped and partly crushed by a falling tree which also broke his spine. He was paralysed from the waist down and died an agonising death.

Konrad Mack drove for less than half a mile when it fell into a fissure that opened. He was burned to death by molten magma that blasted up from the deep. He was the lucky one, being killed within minutes.

There was no one to come to their aid.

****

Twenty-nine

There is a number of large pre-historic caldera formed by extinct volcanoes of huge proportions. The one in Yellowstone Park has been dead since the birth of history.

Then the earth trembled and shook; the foundations of the mountains rocked and quivered........   *(Ps.18: 7)*

The eruption of the "extinct" super-volcano in Wyoming USA, will be the greatest, yet worst volcanic eruption in seventy thousand years. It will be the most enormous explosion tearing away a great segment of the Earth's crust. Its blast so great, it will be heard right around the world, far greater than Krakatoa back in 1883. The immediate devastation will spread north eastward across Montana, South Dakota, Nebraska, Iowa, parts of Minnesota and Illinois and as far east as Chicago.

I looked on the earth - it was a barren waste; at the sky - there was no light. I looked at the mountains - they were shaking and the hills were rocking to-and-fro. I saw there were no people; even the birds had flown away. The fertile land had become a desert; its cities were in ruins. I heard a cry, like a woman in labour, a scream like a woman bearing her first child.   *(Jer: 4.23-31)*

Nothing will have prepared America for the vast devastation that emanates from this massive eruption. It will have literally wiped out farming in the breadbasket of continental North America at a stroke. The area of devastation will be the size of Western Europe.

The consequences will be slightly less immediate but devastatingly worldwide. The first of these effects will be on the world's climate. An estimate of at least one thousand, one hundred and fifty cubic kilometres of debris will have been blasted into the atmosphere. This extraordinary amount, much

209

of it in the form of dust, will be carried on the winds and encircle the globe. Sunlight will be dimmed, global cooling will begin, first in the Northern Hemisphere; then globally evident within a couple of months.

Catastrophic disruption of the world food supply will be the consequence. Crop yields of all kinds across the world will then decline from the lack of sunlight and cooling temperatures. Famine, particularly in the poorer countries will become endemic.

The cooling effect of the volcanic eruption will coincide with the onset of the coldest phase of the 179 year Milankovitch cycle. The Arctic and Antarctic icecaps will creep to ever lower latitudes, year by year. Winters will become more severe. Scientists will voice fears that an ice age could be about to visit the planet, if a critical mass of ice and snow is allowed to cover too much of the globe.

World governments will be panicked into a decision to 'seed' the Arctic and Antarctic icecaps with black discs. The massive airlift will work, albeit very slowly at first. Constant 'top-ups' will be needed as ice and snow re-cover some of the areas already covered. But not over the landmasses of Greenland and the Antarctic continent, due to growing worries about the probable effect on seal levels.

Within five years the spread of the icecaps and glaciers will be seen to be slowing down. Ultimately, a critical mass of ice-cover, from a much-intensified Milankovitch cooling cycle, will have been avoided. The potentially terminal consequences of a global ice age averted.

I destroyed some of you as I destroyed Sodom and Gomorrah. *(Am: 4.11)*

****

210

Thirty

The explosion of an atomic bomb in Israel will be the pivotal event that turns the tide of world history - terrorists will finally become the pariahs. This new horror will be the defining moment for the Jews to undertake the role for which God originally chose them.

I looked at the earth - it was a barren waste; at the sky - there was no light. I looked at the mountains - they were shaking and the hills were rocking to and fro. I saw there were no people; even the birds had flown away. The fertile land had become a desert; its cities were in ruins. (Jer. 4: 23 - 26)

A new worldwide generation of Jews will emerge, influenced by the traumatic experience of their parents and grandparents.

So I am going to take her into the desert again; there I will win her back with words of love. She will respond to me there as she did when she was young, when she came from Egypt.
(Hos. 2: 14 - 15)

****

Cardinals will elect Charles Victor, an Ugandan, as the new Pope. His inaugural address will be a seminal event in religious history. This is that speech of June 3rd that year, on the new 'instant' multi-lingual network: -

"Some of you may wonder why I wished to be known as Pope Charles Victor. The name Charles is in honour of the first Ugandan martyr, Charles Lwanga. The second is in honour of the first African Pope elected in 189 AD, Victor 1st.

I intend to dedicate my short pontificate to reconciliation with the Jews. I start that process now with this address as I know I only have a short time to live!

Some of you will perhaps recall a short passage that comes near the end of St. Luke's gospel when Jesus appeared to His Disciples after his Resurrection. It ends, '...*must be preached to all nations, beginning in Jerusalem.*' I take that statement as my justification for addressing you.

Jeremiah told me, indirectly of course, to tell you to come back to God. *He told me to go and say to Israel, "Unfaithful Israel, come back to me. I am merciful and will not be angry; I will not be angry with you for ever.*   *(Jer. 3: 12)*

The Jewish faith goes back over four thousand years. So I find it difficult to understand why the Jewish faithful have persisted for so long in waiting for the Messiah.

It seems to me that, before the birth of Christ, you could be forgiven for misinterpreting the Messiah of the prophets as a future king, one who would lead you out of oppression under the Romans. But, to continue to believe that Jesus was a prophet for another two thousand and some years, without questioning this belief, is virtually incomprehensible to me!

Your historical suffering, spread over many years, more particularly the atomic bomb, was foretold by the prophet Hosea:

The God I serve will reject his people, because they have not listened to him. They will become wanderers among the nations. I will attack this sinful people and punish them. Nations will join together against them   *(Hos. 9: 17 & 10:10)*

There must surely be a case, after all these years, to re-examine your own scripture in a new light, with a new mind, a new heart and a new spirit. I ask you - no, I plead with all my being, that you might listen with a new ear, to comprehend with a new mind, believe with a new heart, a new faith and new spirit that you do not again do what Jeremiah complained about and reject my plea.

212

"They turned their backs on me; and though I kept on teaching them, they would not listen and learn".   (Jer. 32: 33)

I take courage from the words of your scripture and from the events your nation has suffered. Hosea said, perhaps referring to the devastation of that atomic bomb.

So I am going to take her into the desert again; there I will win her back with words of love. She will respond to me there as she did when she was young, when she came from Egypt. Then once again she will call me her husband.

(Hos. 2: 14 - 16)

When I meditated on these words, I felt em-boldened that given the opportunity, I would speak of such matters. I ask you again, to re-examine your own scriptures so that what Zechariah had to say may come true:

"When that time comes," says the Lord Almighty, "A fountain will be opened to purify the descendants of David."

(Zech. 13: 1)

One final plea. When Jesus went up to Jerusalem for the Passover, St. Luke records that as he came closer to the city of Jerusalem he wept, just as you have done in more recent times.

He came closer to the city and when he saw it, he wept over it... because you did not recognise the time when God came to save you.   (Lk. 19: 41 & 44)

I'll conclude this short address by saying, that if you do as I ask I'm sure God will lead you to the truth, just as St. John wrote.

When, however, the spirit comes, who reveals the truth about God, He will lead you into all the truth.   (Jn. 16: 13)

So may God the Father, the Son and the Holy Spirit be

213

with you and bless you all."

The Pope's assassination will shock the world. Not only because it will occur so soon after his inauguration but also because of its combined impact with his speech. He even alluded to the probable consequences - his death. The media will all agree - the Pope knew he would be killed for what he did, yet he did it! Almost all of them quoted the words of St. John:

"I am telling you the truth: a grain of wheat remains no more than a single grain unless it is dropped into the ground and it dies. If it does, then it produces many more grains"

(Jn. 12: 24)

The Pope's speech will fall on fertile soil amongst some religious Jewish leaders. They will reconsider what led nations to turn against them, from the slavery in Egypt to the last outrage, - the atomic bomb? They will have turned to their scripture in search of answers. The rabbis will find what they seek in passages from Isaiah and Zephaniah and then begin to change their people's attitude.

The holy God of Israel, the Lord who saves you, says: "I am the Lord your God, the one who wants to teach you for your own good and direct you in the way you should go

(Is. 48: 17 - 19)

Sing and shout for joy, people of Israel! Rejoice with all your heart, Jerusalem! The Lord has ended your punishment; he has removed all your enemies. The Lord, the King of Israel, is with you; there is no reason now to be afraid. The Lord your God is with you; his power gives you victory. The Lord will delight in you and his love will give you new life. He will sing and be joyful over you, as joyful as people at a festival."

(Zeph. 3: 13, 15, 17 & 18)

A change to Christianity will gather momentum like a

snowball rolling down a mountainside because God will remove all hindrance as is recorded in the vision of St. John: -

Then I saw an angel coming down from heaven, holding in his hand the key of the abyss and a heavy chain. He seized the dragon, that ancient serpent - that is, the Devil, or Satan - and chained him up for a thousand years. The angel threw him into the abyss, locked it and sealed it, so that he could not deceive the nations any more until the thousand years were over. *(Rev. 20: 1 - 3)*

Increasing numbers of Jews will have the courage to make the change to Christianity - in less than two hundred years, with over 50% of Jews being Catholic, the nation will declare itself a Catholic Country.

Rejoice, O Jerusalem, since through you all men will be gathered together to the Lord. I am coming to gather the people of all nations. When they come together, they will see what my power can do. *(Is. 66: 18)*

The Jews will train and send out teams of missionaries to the nations of the world, preaching Christianity with the fervour of the newly converted.

"Then I will change the people of the nations and they will pray to me alone and not to other gods. They will all obey me. At that time you, my people, will no longer need to be ashamed that you rebelled against me. I will leave there a humbled and lowly people, who will come to me for help. *(Zeph. 3: 9,11 &12)*

The Jewish nation will, at long last, be performing the role for which God chose them. Their prayers will include - *'Be with me while I proclaim your power and might to all generations to come'.* *(Ps. 71: 18)*

God's will on earth shall be accomplished.

Many nations will come streaming to it and their people will say, "Let us go up to the hill of the Lord, to the temple of

215

Israel's God. He will teach us what he wants us to do; we will walk in the paths he has chosen. For the Lord's teaching comes from Jerusalem; from Zion he speaks to his people."

(Is. 2: 2 - 3)

For God had said:

And this Good News about the Kingdom will be preached throughout all the world for a witness to all mankind; and then the end will come. *(Mt. 24: 14)*

****

Thirty-one

The spark that lights the fire of this new endeavour will be the invention of the Ladalev machine. The brainchild of a very bright English student, a few years after leaving university.

When doing research for his thesis, he will chance upon an old paper on the Internet, published by Professors Laithwaite and Dawson. Its title, "Gyroscopic Inertial Propulsion", dated September 1994. He will also have chanced upon another Internet paper in his search – 'Anti-gravity News and Space Drive Technology'- dated July 1997. It contains a list of twenty recommended books of which, via his local library, he will manage to trace and read seven. These will set his inventive genius on fire.

The original models of these first three Ladalev machines (coined from **La**ithwaite & **Da**wson **Lev**itation) will be able to be seen in the Science Museum in London. The first will only have lost weight, the second will have lifted itself but little else, the third will be the first anti-gravity lifting machine. The seemingly impossible made possible.

NASA staff will recognise the opportunity to "drive" into space, carrying a load initially like a van, then like a lorry at a fraction of the cost of rockets! Money will be allocated to pick up the threads of space probe technology from the past but not space travel itself. The driving force will be to determine how best to obtain materials, mainly metals, from our solar system, due to their severe shortage and spiralling cost on Earth. The first Lunar Ladalev will depart - its crew's mission to locate the most suitable Base-Station site, with easy access to ice.

Levitons (as lunar Ladalevs will become known) will take geologists far and wide, in the zero atmosphere and one sixth of Earth's gravity, to prospect for minerals and metals. Six "simple" communication satellites will be put into Moon orbit, to ensure global Lunar communications as well as to provide an essential communication link with Earth even from the far side of the Moon.

The next target will be the asteroids, which will be selected for their content. Those of greatest interest are called Near Earth Asteroids, more than 400 in all. "NEAR Shoemaker" was sent on a reconnaissance mission in 1996, one of its objectives was to prospect for precious chemicals and metals. Earth's longer-term needs had been foreseen even then. When the probe was almost out of fuel in February 2001, NASA 'engineered' a soft landing on a pre-selected asteroid - `Eros`. When it was successfully accomplished, there were indications that 'Eros' might contain £10,000 billion worth of platinum and cobalt and up to £500 billion worth of gold at 2001 prices!

Beyond these first two phases of 'mining in space', past unmanned space probes had already provided the foundation stones of knowledge upon which to plan for inter-planetary sourcing. Searching the viable planets and/or their moons, for the rarer material deposits. This will become the third priority.

The ability to travel very much faster in space will come from a chance event, a fatal accident, an explosion in the Conseil European pour la Recherche Nucleaire (CERN) in Geneva. Scientific investigation will eventually discover the cause of the explosion - the unlocking of the hydrogen atom, converting it back to the pure energy from which it was originally formed. Their work will lead to a whole new branch of physics based on a completely new Atomic Energy Reversion Theory.

Minds will turn to the means of controlling the massive energy release - such that the rate of release can not only be controlled but also directed. The invention of the Hydrogen Energy Reversion Drive, which will become known as the HERD Thruster, will ultimately emerge from their endeavours.

The advent of the HERD Thruster, its initial speed two and a half times that of the Ladalevs, will cut travelling times dramatically. A further twenty years of development will increase speeds to over 500,000 mph, albeit the greater mass of centrifuge ships will mean longer periods of acceleration.

By the end of the millennium, HERD development will enable the solar system to be traversed at speeds of up to fifteen million mph. These speeds will only be reached on the longest journeys as up to five days will have to be spent accelerating and then again, another five days decelerating to keep G-forces within acceptable limits. Neptune, depending on its relative position to Earth, will typically take 10 - 15 days, whereas Mars, Callisto, Rhea and Lepetus will then be only 3 - 5 days away.

The dream of journeying between the planets will have been realised, much like ocean or air travel on earth from country to country, in earlier times.

****

Thirty-two

First of all, you must understand that in these last days some people will appear whose lives are controlled by their own lust. They will mock you and ask, "He promised to come, didn't he? Where is he? Our fathers have already died but everything is still the same as it was since the creation of the world.
(2 Pet. 3: 3 - 4)

The faithful, who rejected Satan's temptations, know in their hearts that death of the body is inevitable anyway but they also know that death cannot kill the soul.

Christ said, in answer to a question from his disciples, referring to all the privation and tests and temptations visited on mankind:

"Soon after the trouble of those days, the sun will grow dark, the moon will no longer shine, the stars will fall from heaven and the powers in space will be driven from their courses.
(Mt. 24: 29)

A distant dot will appear in the night sky - belying its size. It will be a huge body, almost the size of Saturn but nowhere near as beautiful.

From its speed and trajectory tracked by astronomers, an awful truth will dawn upon mankind - it will be an earth-grazer like no other.

It will be a very near miss indeed when it does arrive. Astronomers will have calculated that it will overtake and pass the earth outside earth's normal orbit by just over two million miles, fulfilling Isaiah's prophecy.

The Lord is going to devastate the earth and leave it desolate. He will twist the earth's surface and scatter its people. Everyone will meet the same fate - the priests and the people, slaves and masters, buyers and sellers, lenders and borrowers, rich and poor. *The earth will lie shattered and ruined. The Lord has spoken and it will be done.*

(Is. 24: 1 - 3)

As the heavenly body nears the earth, its gravitational pull will cause a major perturbation of the earth's orbit. Its passage past earth will then only be over one million miles distant. As it overtakes and rushes past, it will seem to fill the sky, its malevolent face lit by the sun. Its gravity pulling the earth still further from its normal orbit round the sun. As it races ahead of the earth, its job will have been done.

Hearts will melt with fear; knees tremble, strength is gone; faces grow pale. *(Nah. 2: 10)*

Its gravitational power very many times that of the moon, will create enormous tidal flows, huge tsunamis wil be generated worldwide, the like of which have only once been seen. They will cause massive coastal destruction and loss of life, smashing away coastal towns and cities, also flooding much of the land. It will have distorted the earth's crust into an ovoid shape, causing the tectonic plates to shift - earthquakes and volcanoes will become commonplace.

And so the earth will quake and everyone on the land will be in distress. The whole earth will be shaken; it will rise and fall like the river Nile. The time is coming when I will make the sun go down at noon and the earth grow dark in daytime.

(Amos. 8: 8 - 9)

In the wake of the malevolent body's passing, earth's orbit will be changed, as will that of the moon's orbit around the earth. The disturbance of the moon will break the precision gyroscopic combination with earth, it will cause the earth's axis to begin to wobble and the stars will no longer appear to be fixed in the night sky.

There will be strange things happening to the sun, the

moon and the stars. On earth whole countries will be in despair, afraid of the roar of the sea and the raging tides. People will faint from fear as they wait for what is coming over the whole earth, for the powers in space will be driven from their courses (Lk. 21: 25 -26)

The huge tides that will have slowed the earth's rate of rotation - the instability of its axis an added nightmare.

The stars, planets, comets and constellations in the heavens seeming to make strange moves across the sky as the earth wobbles ever-more acutely on its axis.

How terrible it will be in those days for women who are pregnant and for mothers with little babies! For the trouble at that time will be far more terrible than any there has ever been, from the beginning of the world to this very day. Nor will there ever be anything like it again. But God has already reduced the number of days; had he not done so, nobody would survive. (Mt. 24: 19 - 21)

Then a bright unearthly light will fill the heavens. *There will be the shout of command; the archangel's voice, the sound of God's trumpet and the Lord himself will come down from heaven.* (1 Thes. 4: 16)

Then will come the most dramatic sound to herald the Lord's coming - *'Veni Emmanuel'*. Christ will make His appearance on judgement day, at the decibel's peak – the final resounding bells of MacMillans masterpiece.

Then the sign of the Son of Man will appear in the sky; and all the peoples of earth will weep as they see the Son of Man coming on the clouds of heaven with power and great glory. The great trumpet will sound and he will send out his angels to the Four Corners of the earth and they will gather his chosen people from one end of the world to the other.

(Mt. 24: 30 - 31)

The assembly of all peoples, of all nations, of all time, will be completed and the sound of Poulenc's '*Gloria*'. It will fill the heavens to honour the appearance and grandeur of Christ sitting on His seat of judgement.

The glory of the Lord will be magnified by the sound of the '*Dies Ire*' from Berlioz requiem, played by an orchestra of hundreds and sung by a choir of thousands.

"Then he will divide them into two groups, just as a shepherd separates the sheep from the goats. He will put the righteous people on his right and the others on his left. Then the King will say to the people on his right, 'come, you who are blessed by my father! Come and possess the kingdom which has been prepared for you ever since the creation of the world.

Then he will say to those on his left, Away from me, you that are under God's curse! Away to the eternal fire which has been prepared for the Devil and his angels!"

(Mt. 25: 32, 34,41)

God's cursed will despair as they hear the sound of Messiaen's '*Quatuor pour le fin de Temps*'. It will reflect their soul's broken spirit when they realize the utter timelessness of Christ's verdict as they are discarded into hell's eternity.

Acknowledgments

I wish to express my sincere thanks to the following people, each of whom contributed greatly to the whole – Molly Burkett, Jayne Thompson, Alan and Eve, for their valued comments, suggestions and the encouragement of a tyro.

I also wish to thank Ursula Schneider of the Swiss Embassy, the Solothurn tourist office, Mr David Balfour of the Maidenhead library and its staff and for the unstinting support of Andrew Scadding.

Additionally I wish to thank the authors of the following books and the articles contributed to magazines, papers and the Internet, all of whom provided additional valued background material.

Astronomy Data Book – Robinson and Muirden
Catchism of the Catholic Church – G Chapman
Chronicle of the Popes – P G Maxwell-Stuart
Chronicle of the 20th Century – Chronicle Communications Ltd
Dictionary of the Third Reich – Penguin
Encarta 2000 – Microsoft Corporation
Encyclopaedia of the Earth – Hutchinson
Energy : The Solar-Hydrofen Alternative – JOM Bockris
Faster than the Speed of Light – Joao Magueijo
Guinness Book of Astronomy – Patrick Moore
Guinness Encyclopaedia of the Living World
State of the World – G Gardner and P Sampat
The Cambridge Encyclopaedia of Human Evolution
The Daily Telegraph
The Evolving Continents – Brian Windley
The Good News Bible – Collins
The New Atlas of the Universe – Patrick Moore
The New Jerusalem Bible – Darton, Longman & Todd Ltd
The Origin of Human Kind – Stephen Thomkins
The Spectator
The Sunday Telegraph
The Tablet
The Times Concise Atlas of the World
The Weather Book – M Joseph Ltd

Cover Picture: A painting of the Verena Gorge, its hermitage and chapels, by an unknown artist in the early 1900s